NUTS

A novel by

KACY COOK

MARSHALL CAVENDISH CHILDREN

Marshall Cavendish Corporation
99 White Plains Road
Tarrytown, NY 10591
www.marshallcavendish.us/kids

This book is a work of fiction. Names, characters, places, and incidents are products of the author's imagination and are used fictitiously. Any resemblance to actual events or locales or persons, living or dead, is entirely coincidental.

Library of Congress Cataloging-in-Publication Data
Cook, Kacy.
Nuts / by Kacy Cook. — 1st ed.
p. cm.
Summary: When eleven-year-old Nell finds a tiny baby squirrel on the ground in her yard, she begs her parents to let her raise it as a pet, even after the research she does shows that this is not a good idea.
ISBN 978-0-7614-5652-0
[1. Squirrels—Fiction. 2. Animals—Infancy—Fiction. 3. Wildlife rescue—Fiction. 4. Family life—Ohio—Fiction. 5. Ohio—Fiction.] I.
Title.
PZ7.C76983Nu 2010
[Fic]—dc22
2009004354

Book design by Becky Terhune
Editor: Robin Benjamin

Printed in China (E)
First edition
10 9 8 7 6 5 4 3 2 1

Marshall Cavendish
Children

For Leah, Jacob, and Ben

ONE

Sometimes even a tiny noise can bug you. Like a dripping faucet or a creaky door hinge. Especially when it doesn't stop. And if you don't know what's making the sound, it can really drive you nuts.

I had a day that began with a noise, one I probably wouldn't even have noticed if I had heard it only once or twice. But when I think back on it now—on that day, that special day—I still remember the pesky little sound that started it all.

I was at my desk answering e-mail from my best friend, Greta. The clock on my computer screen read 9:00 a.m. on the button, March 20—the first day of spring—when I noticed something squeaking. It was faint, and it didn't really bother me . . . until it happened again and again and again. I couldn't figure out where it was coming from, and before long I couldn't think of anything else.

I looked in my hamsters' cage, but Gus and Harry were burrowed into the wood shavings, asleep. There was nothing under my bed. Well, there was an empty tissue box, my diary from when I was ten, one tennis shoe, and some dust bunnies—but nothing that squeaked. When I pressed my ear to the wall, I heard only the quiet rumble of the furnace.

Finally, I crossed the hall to my brothers' room, where they were playing Scrabble.

Jack was sitting on the edge of his unmade bed, throwing a baseball into the glove he was trying to break in. I knew right away that he was losing to Charley. The bill of Jack's Cleveland Indians cap was pulled down almost to the tip of his nose. Unless he's in church or at the dinner table, Jack wears that hat, and whenever he's upset, angry, or annoyed, he tugs at it. I could tell he'd been tugging away.

Charley was sitting on the floor, studying his letters with a big grin on his face. He got up on his knees and spilled tiles onto the board, which was balanced on top of their wastebasket.

"The blank one is a *B*," he said as he arranged the letters: Z-O-M-__-I-E.

Charley is only seven, but he's a really good Scrabble player. For one thing, he's a better speller than I am, and I'm nearly twelve. Dad calls him Robokid because he spells like he has a dictionary programmed into his brain.

"And it's a double-word score! Let's see, that's ten, eleven"— Charley held up his fingers to help out—"twelve, thirteen, fourteen, fifteen, sixteen. And sixteen times two is . . . What's sixteen times two, Nell?" he asked when he saw me standing in the doorway.

"Thirty-two," I said. I'm still better than he is at math.

"Thirty-two points! Woo-hoo!" he cheered. "What's my score now?"

"Man!" Jack threw himself backward on the bed and pulled his cap all the way over his face. Jack is nine and hates losing to anybody, but especially to Charley. "Let's play something else," he grumbled.

"Hey, you guys, come listen to this," I said.

"What is it?" asked Charley.

"You tell me."

Jack jumped up to follow me.

"Wait! It's your turn," Charley called after him. "You're quitting!"

"No, I'm helping Nell," Jack said.

"You have to be quiet 'cause it's not very loud," I half-whispered when we reached my room. We waited in silence. It was maybe twenty or thirty seconds before I heard it again. "There! Did you hear that?"

"What?" asked Charley, who had just arrived. "I don't hear anything."

"Shhhh. Listen. . . . There it is again."

"Is it like *eee . . . eee?*" Jack mimicked the sound.

"Yeah! What do you think it is?"

"I don't know," he said, walking around the room.

Charley opened the door to my closet and looked inside. Jack checked out my computer. I got down on my hands and knees and put my ear to the floor.

"Hey! I think it's outside." Jack pulled back the curtains. The window was open a crack.

"Look! Could it be coming from that?" Charley pointed to something moving on the patch of dirt beneath our tire swing, which hangs from a tall ash tree in our backyard.

"Man!" Jack said. "What the heck is it?"

We ran downstairs for a better look. Even from the dining room window, we couldn't recognize the animal. But whatever it was, it was rolling around in the dirt, making pitiful cries.

"It must be hurt," I said softly.

"Do something, Nell," begged Charley, who is the most tenderhearted of the three of us.

"Maybe we should check it out," I told them.

The screen door banged shut behind us as we raced outside. But as we got close to the tree, I told the boys to slow down. I knew an injured animal—even a small one—might try to bite.

We crouched behind the tree and peeked around. At the base of the trunk, there was an almost-hairless creature, squirming with all its might, still crying out every now and then.

One glimpse of its face erased all my fears.

"Aww, it's only a baby." I walked around the tree and knelt beside it. The boys quietly joined me. "See? Its eyes are still closed."

Once Greta's cat had kittens, and their eyelids were sealed like that when they were first born.

"Is it a baby rat?" Charley whispered.

"I think it's a squirrel," I said, but I was guessing, too. The animal—about the size of a pinecone from our blue spruce tree— had so little fur that it was hard to tell what it was. It did have a long, smooth tail like a rat. But I'd never seen a rat in our yard, and there were always squirrels.

"How do you think it got here?" asked Charley.

"I guess it fell out of the tree," I said.

Charley clapped his hands over his eyes, as if he were trying to block out the image of the falling baby.

But Jack was impressed. "And it's still alive! Wow! How far do you think it fell?"

We tried to spot a nest in the limbs overhead.

"Do squirrels' nests look like birds' nests?" Jack asked. He had recently chipped a front tooth, and when he said words with the letter S, there was a slight whistling sound.

"Beats me," I said. "But I don't see anything that looks like a nest at all. Do you?"

"Maybe it's in the trunk of the tree."

"Yeah, I guess so."

"I think the baby is cold," said Charley. His green eyes were wide.

The temperature wasn't that chilly, but there was a pretty strong breeze. I struggled to keep my long hair out of my face.

"Can we take it inside, Nell?" Charley pleaded, trying to protect the animal from the wind with his legs.

Mom is a part-time accountant with an office in our house, and she sometimes has to be away for business appointments—like she was that morning. She'd left me in charge, but I didn't think this was something I should decide on my own. Besides, what did I know about taking care of a baby whatever-it-was? Even if I did feel sorry for it.

"We'd better wait till Mom gets home," I said. "I don't think she'd like us bringing a wild animal, even a baby one, into the house without asking first."

"Call her cell phone," said Charley.

"We can't bother her for something like this while she's working. What if we interrupt a big meeting?"

"She said we should call if there's an emergency," Charley insisted.

"I think she meant something like a fire or a broken arm. How is this an emergency?"

"It's an emergency for the squirrel, isn't it?" Jack joined in.

Jack loves to argue. He once debated with me about whether or not I enjoy playing volleyball. I couldn't convince him I knew better than he did. I had to give him a really good argument now, or I'd never hear the end of it.

"Yeah, but if it just fell out of its nest, we have to give its mother time to come and get it," I told him. "I think that's even a law or something."

"Man!" Jack tugged at his baseball cap.

Charley got a handful of seeds from one of the birdfeeders in our yard. He piled them on the ground next to the baby. "Squirrels are always eating out of birdfeeders," he explained. Next, he dragged a picnic bench over and laid it on its side to shield the baby from the wind. Besides being really smart for his age, Charley is thoughtful. He had ideas to help the squirrel, while Jack and I hadn't come up with any.

We sat on the screened porch at the back of our house, where we could watch over the baby but we wouldn't frighten off the mother squirrel. We waited to see which mother would show up first—the squirrel's or ours. Jack tugged on his hat, and Charley bit his fingernails. I twisted strands of my hair around and around my index fingers.

"You guys didn't touch it, did you?" I asked after a few minutes. "I've heard wild animals won't go near another animal that has a human smell on it. Not even their own baby."

"I didn't," said Jack.

"Me, either," said Charley.

"You don't smell human, anyway," Jack teased Charley.

"No, *you* don't."

"*You* don't."

"*You* smell like—"

"Okay, okay," I said. "Be quiet or you'll scare the mother away."

So we sat and watched. And waited and waited.

Suddenly Jack jumped up. "Man! There's Wendell!"

"Oh, no!" I cried.

Not that stupid cat. Not now!

TWO

Wendell is a big orange cat that belongs to the Fleagles, who live a few houses down. Wendell has a scar over one eye and patches of missing fur, so I think he must get into a lot of fights. Plus, he hunts smaller animals. Constance Fleagle, who is Jack's age, sometimes calls us over to see a bird or mouse that Wendell has caught and killed. Constance thinks that's funny. We don't.

Wendell was in the yard next door. His ears were perked up. He must have heard the squirrel's cries. My heart pounded as I jumped down the porch stairs, all four in one leap, and ran to the baby.

Jack and Charley took off after Wendell, yelling and waving their arms. The noise was enough to make him run in the opposite direction. The boys chased him down the street.

The baby looked so helpless lying there on the ground. I wished I had a better plan besides just waiting.

"We scared the heck out of Wendell," Charley said as they ran back into our yard.

"Enough that he won't come back?"

"Not for a while, anyway. He ran up a tree!"

"But what if a big dog comes by here?" Jack asked. "What would we do then?"

"Jack! Don't scare Charley," I warned. But it was too late.

"Let's take it inside *right now!*" Charley said. He bit a knuckle to keep from crying.

"Not yet. It'll be all right, Charley. We'll keep watch," I said. "I'm sure its mom will come back soon." But I wasn't sure at all. And I couldn't stand to think of the tiny creature being snatched up by Wendell—or worse.

Except for old Mrs. Brumley, who lives next door and definitely wouldn't want to touch anything "dirty" or "germy" like a wild animal, there weren't any neighbors home that time of day. We're homeschooled or we'd have been away, too. It seemed that we were on our own.

Jack stood on a chair, keeping a lookout. Charley gnawed on his fingernails. I walked back and forth on the porch, twisting my hair and listening to the baby's cries, until I just couldn't stand any more. After Wendell's visit, it did seem more like an emergency. What good would it do to wait for the mother squirrel to come back if the baby wasn't okay when she got there?

"It's time to call Mom," I said.

"Yes!" Jack jumped down from the chair.

Charley stood watch over the baby while Jack and I scrambled to get to the kitchen phone first. Now that the decision was made, we were both bursting to tell Mom the news. Jack beat me by a mile. He grabbed the phone and pressed three to speed dial Mom's cell. I ran upstairs to get on the other phone.

" . . . and Charley thought it was a rat or something," Jack was saying as I picked up, "but Nell thinks it's a baby squirrel."

"I bet Nell is right," Mom said. "It makes sense that squirrels would have babies in the spring, and sometimes they fall out of their nests. Is it hurt?"

"It's not bleeding," I said. "But it's crying a lot and squirming all around."

"Charley gave it some seeds so it won't starve," Jack told her.

"Well, it can't eat seeds yet. If its eyes are sealed closed, it must still be nursing." I remembered that's how it was for Greta's kittens.

"Can we bring it in the house?" asked Jack.

"Did you give the mother plenty of time to come? That would be the best thing for it."

"We've waited and waited," Jack said.

Then I told Mom about Wendell.

"Okay, I guess you'd better bring the baby inside till we can figure out what else to do," she said. "Maybe you should try to give it some warm water. See if you can find an eyedropper. And add some sugar—but just a tiny bit."

Mom said she'd be home soon. Before hanging up, she reminded us, "You have to keep Dotty and Murphy"—our dog and cat—"away from it, too. We don't know how they might react to a strange animal."

Jack and Charley sat on the ground next to the baby while I ran to get something to put it in. I couldn't find a cardboard box, so I took a small drawer from an old dresser in the basement and lined it with a flannel nightgown I'd outgrown. Then I made a quick stop in the bathroom to pull my hair into a ponytail, out of my face.

On my way back outside, I remembered about not getting my human smell on the squirrel. I didn't want to take any chances in case the mother showed up later. And, worse yet, what if the baby peed on me? I grabbed some rubber gloves from the kitchen before joining the boys under the tree.

I knelt down and pulled on the gloves.

"Do you want me to do it?" Jack asked when I didn't pick the squirrel up right away. "I'm not afraid."

"I'm not afraid, either," I lied. "But what if I drop it? It's wiggling so much."

"It already fell out of a tree, stupid!" said Jack. "How much worse could it get?"

"Shut up!" was the best answer I could come up with.

I slipped one hand under the small body and cupped my other hand over it. Then I nestled the squirrel into the folds of the nightgown.

Charley tucked one of the sleeves around the baby, and Jack carried the drawer to the screened porch, where it would be safe. Then we ran to find our pets.

Our black-and-brown-and-white cocker spaniel, Dotty Dimples (who Mom named for the brown "freckles" on her nose), was sleeping by the front door, where she always is when Mom isn't home, waiting for her to return. Dotty is pretty old, and she can't hear or see very well. But to be on the safe side—after all, she can still smell—we closed the French doors that lead to the entryway.

Our cat was trickier to find. Murphy likes to sleep in out-of-the-way places, under furniture or inside cupboards or drawers that are left open. Jack finally found her in a basket of laundry next to the dryer. We closed the basement door and ran to bring the squirrel inside.

We put the drawer in the middle of the kitchen floor and huddled around it.

"We should give it some water," I said, trying to act like I knew what I was doing. I found an eyedropper in a kitchen drawer and put it in some boiling water. I remembered Mom sterilizing bottle nipples this way when Charley was a baby, and it seemed like a good idea now. I mixed a few pinches of sugar, as Mom had suggested, in a small bowl of the boiled water and let it cool.

I pulled back the sleeve covering the baby. The squeaking and squirming had stopped, but we could see that it was still breathing. I looked it over carefully for the first time. I'd never seen a wild animal up close. It was about five inches long, not counting the tail, and had a little bit of dark golden fur. Its eyes were tightly sealed, and even its ears were rolled closed. I could see tiny black toenails.

"Man! Do you think Mom and Dad will let us keep it?" asked Jack. "It doesn't seem like its mother is coming back."

I had been having the same thought, and I liked the idea. I imagined a cute little squirrel with a big fluffy tail coming when I called it and climbing onto my shoulder.

"That would be sweet," I said. "I don't know anyone who has a pet squirrel."

"What should we name it?" asked Charley.

"I wonder if it's a girl or boy," I said. With a gloved finger, I rolled the squirrel onto its back. "I think it's a girl, but I'm not positive."

Jack suggested we name it after Sam, a young squirrel in the book *Redwall*, which Dad had been reading to us at night. "If it's a girl, we'll call her Samantha."

Charley and I agreed that was a pretty good plan.

Charley filled the dropper with warm sugar water and handed it to me. I placed the tip to the baby's mouth, but it wouldn't take any of the liquid. I tried again, but it turned its head away.

"Maybe the water's too hot," said Charley.

I tested a drop on my arm, just like Mom used to do with baby bottles. "No, I don't think so." I was guessing, but I didn't want the boys to know that. At least the water didn't burn me.

"Maybe there's not enough sugar," said Charley.

"Maybe," I said. "Hey! I have an idea. I'll be back in a few minutes. You two watch the squirrel, but don't pick it up."

"Why not?" asked Jack. "It's not yours."

"Just don't," I said. "Remember about human smells. What if we have to put it back outside later?"

"I'll wear the gloves."

"NO! Let it sleep, Jack. It was squirming and crying for a long time, and it's probably tired. Charley, tell me if Jack picks it up."

"Man!" Jack said. "Where are you going, anyway?"

"I'm getting on my computer to see if I can find out what to do."

I ran to my room. I love doing research, and I'm pretty good at it. My dad thinks it's an important part of our homeschooling, and he always tests my skills. I especially like searching the Web. There is so much out there! Dad monitors where I go on the Internet and who I send e-mail to, but he agrees that online research is a valuable tool.

I began a search on squirrels. There were millions of results. I found sites for people who love squirrels, for people who hate squirrels, for people who want to get rid of squirrels. Even sites for ways to cook squirrels!

There were many Web sites with general information, and if I'd had more time, I would have checked out lots of them. But I was in a hurry, so I chose one with a name I liked: Nuts for Squirrels.

I quickly looked around the site until I saw the words *If You Find an Orphaned Squirrel*.

"Perfect!"

I clicked the link. At the top of the page was a notice in a red box:

> If you find a baby squirrel on the ground and there is no sign of the mother after two hours, or if the baby is injured, take it to a licensed wildlife rehabilitator. A veterinarian can help in locating one.

No, no, no, I thought. I didn't know what a "rehabilitator" was, but I knew I didn't want one. I didn't want to give the squirrel to someone else. That notice had to be for people who didn't want to take care of a squirrel themselves. I wanted little Sam or Samantha. I skipped down the page, looking for things I could do on my own.

And there it was—a section on emergency care you could provide until you could get the animal to a "proper caretaker."

As I pressed the key to print, I heard Jack call, "Mom's home!"

THREE

When I got to the kitchen, the boys were practically jumping up and down as they showed off the squirrel. Mom was wearing a navy-blue skirt and jacket—her best work clothes—but she still sat down on the floor next to it.

"Wow!" she said. "Isn't that something?"

Mom loves all animals, but especially wild ones. We live near a ravine, so it's not unusual to see wild animals, like raccoons or even deer, in the yard. Mom gets excited every single time. Once a skunk showed up, and Mom sat looking out the window like I would sit watching my favorite TV show.

"If you want to pick it up, I was using these," I said, handing her the rubber gloves.

"I'm so glad you thought of that, Nell," she said. "I'm not sure if it's good for us *or* for the squirrel if we touch it."

"Do you think it's a boy or a girl?" Charley asked. "Nell thinks it's a girl."

Mom rolled the squirrel over. "Yep, Nell is right."

"Her name is Samantha, then," Charley said. Jack and I nodded our heads.

"We can't get her to eat anything," I told Mom.

"Let me try," she said.

She reheated the sugar water in the microwave, tested the temperature on the back of her hand, and put on the gloves. She held the dropper to Samantha's mouth. Mom tried several times, but Samantha wouldn't take any water from her, either. "We have to figure out something pretty fast," she said. "A tiny baby like this can't go too long without eating."

I told her about the emergency information I'd found online. "It's printing."

"Another good idea, Nell," Mom said. "Now where are we going to keep this baby?"

"We can keep her in our room," Charley offered.

"No way," I said. "I could put her next to my hamsters."

"How about if we put her in the bathroom next to the kitchen?" Mom suggested, meaning our small half-bath. "She'll be warm and safe from Dotty and Murphy there."

"But there's no window," Charley said. "It's dark in there."

"She can't see yet, anyway," I said.

"Well, when she *can* see, are we going to leave the light on all the time?" Charley asked.

"She probably won't be here long enough for us to worry about the light," Mom said.

The boys and I looked at each other. We didn't like the sound of that.

"What if we want to keep her?" Charley asked.

"I was afraid you guys might be thinking something like that." Mom put the drawer with Samantha in it on the bathroom floor and closed the door.

"What's wrong with that?" Jack demanded.

"There are probably dozens of reasons not to do it," Mom

said. "But we'll talk about that later when your father gets home. Let's not get too far ahead of ourselves."

I went to get the information off my printer. I noticed an e-mail address for the person who ran the Web site. A note said her name was Libby and that she had raised squirrels from the "pinkie"—or newborn—stage.

I wanted to ask Libby to be my adviser. If I had experienced help, Mom and Dad might let us keep Samantha. I wondered if Libby was a wildlife rehabilitator and would just tell me again that I had to take Samantha to one. I had to make her think that wasn't possible. I sent this message:

> Dear Libby,
>
> I found a baby squirrel near my house, and I saw your Web site when I was looking for information on what to do. I read the notice about taking it to a wildlife rehabilitator, but unfortunately I live way, way out in the country and there isn't one within miles and miles. Would you PLEASE help me take care of this poor animal? I am following your instructions for emergency care.
>
> Sincerely,
>
> Nell

I grabbed the pages from my printer and hurried downstairs to show the others.

Using the descriptions and pictures from the Web site, we figured that Samantha was about two weeks old. We also learned it is dangerous to feed a baby squirrel that is not warm and the baby would need help staying warm until its eyes opened.

"It's a good thing we found out before it was too late," Mom said. "We can use a heating pad or hot-water bottle to get Samantha warm." I was glad to hear her call the squirrel by name.

The first thing to do, according to the site, was to look for signs of injuries or illness—scratches, cuts, crooked bones, swelling, or trouble breathing—or parasites, such as fleas or maggots.

Mom and I checked the baby all over, including in her mouth and ears. We didn't see any of those problems.

We also needed to check for dehydration. To test, I had to pinch the skin between Samantha's shoulders gently. If it didn't fall back immediately, that was a sign she didn't have enough water in her body. When I grasped Samantha's skin, it bunched up, then sank very slowly back into place.

"That doesn't look good," Mom said.

"We'll have to get something called Pedialyte," I read from the printouts, "and give her some every fifteen minutes for the next hour or two until the dehydration is better."

"We'll get it at the grocery store right away," Mom said.

"Later on—in a day or two—we can give her this other stuff. See?"

"This is great information, Nell. Is that all?" Mom asked.

"No, there's more. Let's see. . . . It also says that a baby squirrel can't—can't—can't . . . What?! Oooh no-o-o-o," I groaned. I dropped the paper and put my hands over my face. "This is *really* not good."

"What's wrong?" asked Charley.

"I thought checking for maggots was bad," I said. "Listen to this: 'A baby squirrel can't excrete waste by itself. The mother squirrel licks the baby to start the process. You will have to stimulate elimination by gently wiping over the baby's genitals'"—I could feel my face growing hot as I read this—"'with a tissue or cotton ball EVERY time you feed the squirrel. This is VERY important or the baby will become bloated and ill and could die.'"

I looked at the boys to see if they were as grossed out as I was.

"What does that mean?" asked Charley.

"It means a baby squirrel can't go to the bathroom by itself," I said. "We have to make Samantha pee and poop or she'll die!"

"Sick!" said Jack. "Do you think that's why her mother pushed her out of the nest?"

"Be serious," I said.

"I *am* serious."

"For goodness' sake!" Mom laughed. "You're making too much of this."

"Maybe you can do that part," I said. "It's a mom thing."

"Okay," she said. "I'll make a deal with you: I'll take care of the bathroom duties—*for now!*—and you guys can tell Dad you've invited a rodent into our home."

It sounded like Mom wouldn't mind us keeping Samantha. But she was right: Dad would not be thrilled. It's not that Dad doesn't like animals; he's just not crazy about having them in the house. Even with our pets, he can never get used to the noises (barking or squeaky hamster wheels in the middle of the night), the messes (animal hair on furniture and clothes, squishy hairballs under bare feet), or the smells. Especially the smells. He really wouldn't be happy about a squirrel—a rodent, as Mom said—in the house.

"*You* can tell him," Jack said to me.

"I think we should all tell him together," I said, "so he knows that we—"

Mom joined in, "—will do *all* the work, and he'll *never* even know the animal is in the house." It was exactly what I was going to say. "He's heard that one before," Mom added.

I knew—we all knew—that she was talking about the hamsters especially. I suddenly wished we'd been better about cleaning their cage, as well as Murphy's litter box, without being told.

"We *will* do all the work," I said, but with less confidence than when I started the sentence.

"Uh-huh," Mom said. "Now, did the Web site say what you should do with Samantha if you can't take care of her yourself?"

"Not really," I said.

I knew that I should have mentioned the part about the wildlife rehabilitator, but I didn't even know what a wildlife rehabilitator was or if there was one in our town. It was way too soon to mention that—and I was afraid Mom would try to find one.

"This may be a whole lot harder than you guys imagine," Mom said. "And I'm not just talking about your father. How often does the baby have to be fed?"

I checked the instructions. "After the dehydration is better, we'll have to feed her every three hours."

"Think about that!" Mom said. "And what about the bathroom problem? How could you children possibly do all of this and keep up with your other work? I know how you guys feel, but I just don't see how this can be good for you or the baby."

I didn't know what to say. I only knew that I wanted to try to care for Samantha.

Being homeschooled should help, I thought. I wasn't always homeschooled. When I was in first grade, we lived in a big city and I went to a big school. But Mom and Dad wanted to "simplify" our lives, so we moved to this small town, Meadowlake, Ohio. Mom began working from home and learned about homeschooling. I haven't gone to regular school since. My brothers have never been.

There is a lot I like about being homeschooled—especially that we get to travel and I can spend more time playing the piano, reading, or poking around on the computer—but at that moment, I *loved* being homeschooled. There wouldn't be any way to raise a baby squirrel if I went to a regular school all day.

"Let's do what we can," Mom said. "We have some good instructions here, so we'll get busy with these until we figure out what to do next."

We took a large plastic bottle from the recycling bin and filled it with hot water. Mom wrapped it in an old T-shirt and hooked a piece of the hem around the drawer knob to keep it from rolling onto the baby. She placed the bottle in the drawer next to Samantha. Then we went to the grocery.

When we returned, I heated a little of the Pedialyte and tested it on my wrist. It was supposed to be "body temperature," I had learned, meaning I should barely be able to feel it when I put a drop on my skin. It was just right, I thought.

I put the gloves on and cradled the tiny baby in my left palm. I already felt much more comfortable holding her. I filled the eyedropper with my right hand and put the tip to Samantha's mouth.

"Please eat," I whispered as I squeezed the rubber top.

Samantha began drinking the liquid—almost the whole dropperful. The boys clapped and cheered.

As she'd promised, Mom then took a tissue and wiped it over Samantha's lower parts—as the boys and I looked away. But the baby didn't go to the bathroom.

"I think I'm doing this right," Mom said. "She probably

doesn't have to go yet because she's been dehydrated. We'll try again later. But I just don't know about this," she added. "There are so many things that can go wrong, and we have to consider what is best for the squirrel. We'd better think of a Plan B. Just in case things don't go the way we hope."

FOUR

I couldn't wait for Greta to get home from school. Greta lives across the street, and we've been best friends for almost five years. I could just imagine how surprised she was going to be when she saw Samantha. I sent her an e-mail saying to come over as soon as possible.

At 3:15, I heard the squealing brakes of the school bus coming to a stop a block away. Right on time.

Twenty minutes later, the doorbell rang. Mom let Greta in and pointed her toward the kitchen.

"Look!" I announced. "It's a baby squirrel!"

"Oh my gosh! It's so tiny!" Greta said. "Where did you get it? Where's its mother? Are you going to keep it?"

I told her all about our day. Well, I didn't tell her *everything*. I didn't tell Greta about wildlife rehabilitators, either.

"Is it a boy or girl?" she asked. "Does it have a name?"

"Her name is Samantha."

"You're so lucky," Greta said. Then after thinking for a few seconds, she added, "But do you know if Wendell came down from the tree? I'd sure hate to be around if Constance finds him, especially if she finds out how he got there."

Constance Fleagle is a spoiled brat. She always, always, *always* gets her way. She pouts or throws a fit until her parents do whatever she wants. And it could definitely cause trouble for us if Constance whined about the boys chasing Wendell up a tree—even if it were for a good reason—just because my dad hates to deal with Mr. Fleagle. If the Fleagles were involved in any way, it might be yet another reason for Dad to say we couldn't keep Samantha.

But Greta and I didn't let that problem stop us from making plans about Samantha's future as my pet. I said I was going to train her to sit on my shoulder while I fed her peanuts. Greta said she would help me to raise her and take care of her whenever I was away from home.

"Maybe we could teach her to do tricks," I said. "I saw a squirrel on TV once that water-skied in a swimming pool behind a toy motorboat."

"I saw a chicken on YouTube that played a little piano."

"We'll train her to do something completely different. Maybe kite-flying."

"Horseback riding!"

"Ping-Pong!"

"Skateboarding!"

We were rolling on the floor laughing, but it was giving me ideas. A squirrel would be the greatest pet ever. Dad just *had* to let me keep Samantha.

It was time to give Samantha more Pedialyte, and I enjoyed showing Greta what I had learned. I heated some of the liquid, put on the rubber gloves, and gently picked up the squirrel.

"Here, wittle Mantha," I whispered in baby talk.

"Mantha!" Greta laughed. "I like that."

I did, too.

When Greta's mother called to remind her that she had homework waiting, Greta didn't want to leave. She promised to come back every day.

"Good luck with your dad," she said on her way out the door.

Dad got home from work at dinnertime, and we ran to meet him on the driveway with the story of our rescue.

"Guess what?" Charley began. "Nell heard a noise, and—"

"We found a baby squirrel!" said Jack. "Her mother's probably dead or something."

"I've been doing research—" I tried to get a word in.

"Can we keep her?" asked Jack.

It was easy to tell that Dad wasn't as thrilled about the news as we were.

"I don't want to disappoint you guys," he said, "but wild animals are very difficult for humans to raise. It could die. I know you kids wouldn't want that."

This wasn't the argument we were expecting.

"Man!"

"We'll talk about it tonight," said Dad. "Now let's get cleaned up for dinner."

After we ate, we gathered in the living room, like we do almost every night for Dad to read to us. But this time we had a meeting about the squirrel. I made sure that Dotty and Murphy couldn't get into the room, and I put the drawer in front of the couch so Dad could see the baby.

"Her name is Mantha," I said.

"It's *Sa*-mantha!" Jack jumped up. "Don't change her name without asking us!"

"Don't get all excited," I said. "Mantha is just a nickname."

Jack opened his mouth to say something else, but Dad broke in, "If you're going to fight over this already, we can end our meeting right now."

"Mantha is okay with me," Jack said grumpily. He plopped onto a chair and tugged the bill of his cap. I was glad that, for once, he knew better than to argue.

"You kids tell me your side first," Dad said. "Nell, do you want to start?"

Knowing how much Dad loves research, I told him what I'd already found out online about raising baby squirrels. "There's a Web site called Nuts for Squirrels with a lady named Libby who has raised squirrels. She said she'd tell me everything I need to know," I said, even though I hadn't heard back yet from Libby.

"That's fine, and I'll want to hear more about this Libby," Dad said, "but don't forget the library, Nell. Sometimes I think you're too reliant on that computer. Now what about you boys?"

"We're helping," Jack said. "We protected her from Wendell, and we want to learn stuff, too."

"Samantha . . . I mean Mantha," Charley said, glancing at me, "doesn't have anybody but us." He hugged his arms to his chest and looked up at Dad. If anything could melt Dad's heart, it would be the sweet but serious look on Charley's face. His eyes looked about twice as big as normal.

Dad sat shaking his head. He ran his fingers over his short, dark hair. Then he got up and walked back and forth across the living room. He cracked his knuckles. He looked out the window. None of us said a word. Finally, Dad sat back down, covered his face with his hands, and sighed deeply. But he still didn't say anything.

Mom spoke up: "I've been thinking about it all day, and maybe this would be a good project for the kids. Of course, the squirrel's well-being comes first, but wouldn't this be a wonderful study in natural science? They've already learned a good deal from the experience, and it sounds like Nell has an expert who will help them. They showed a lot of initiative and independence today in saving the animal's life. And it would be only until the squirrel could live on its own. It wouldn't be a danger to the kids while it's small."

Dad sat quietly a little bit longer, and then he said, "I think I may be outnumbered here." He smiled to show us he wasn't mad. "I want you all to know that I understand why the idea of raising a baby squirrel sounds interesting and fun. But I don't want us to forget what is at stake here. There are so many things that are important in your lives and learning. Schoolwork and music and art and sports, plus all the places we like to go. I don't want to see all of your time going to one thing, which could happen when you are taking care of a very small creature."

"It's only for a little while," I said.

"I know, Nell. I'm trying to remember that. The other thing I want to mention is that kids can lose interest in things—it's only natural—and this isn't a project where you can just stop in the middle. Your mother and I are too busy to pick up the slack if that happens."

"And there's another problem I thought of," Mom added. "You can't get too attached to the squirrel. Someday, you will have to let her go. That can be a difficult thing to do."

"That's exactly right," Dad said. "Do you all understand these issues?"

We nodded, but none of us spoke.

Then, using a stern voice, Dad said, "I'm willing to give this a try. But this is a very big responsibility. You have to prove you can handle it. And it has to be understood that this project will end just as soon as the squirrel can care for itself. Wild animals are not pets."

Dad paused for a few seconds. I think he couldn't believe he was about to agree to let another animal into the house.

"I'll give you a trial period of one week," he said. "But, at any time, if I think this animal is getting anything less than great care, it's over. Does everyone understand that?"

"Yes!" Jack, Charley, and I all yelled at once.

I jumped to my feet.

"One week," Dad repeated.

We were determined to do a good job. And I was sure that, if everything went well, we could convince Mom and Dad that wild animals *could* be pets. But I'd have to think about that later. At the moment, I had plenty of other problems: keeping up with round-the-clock feedings, learning more about caring for Mantha, hoping Mom wouldn't get sick of the bathroom duties, and making sure there were no bad messes or smells that would cause Dad to change his mind.

But my biggest worry of all was that Mom and Dad would find out about wildlife rehabilitators.

FIVE

Even though Mom and I got up several times during the night to look after the squirrel, I still woke really early the next morning. That's something I never do. But I just couldn't wait to see Mantha.

I heated some Pedialyte and went to check on her in the bathroom. She was sleeping, snuggled against the hot-water bottle. We decided against using a heating pad because Mom was afraid the baby wouldn't be able to get away from it if she got too warm, plus there were the dangers of leaving it plugged in all the time. I refilled the bottle every time I fed Mantha.

I lightly rubbed my index finger over the top of Mantha's head. She stretched and yawned. I picked her up and held her to my cheek.

"How's it going?" Mom asked from the doorway.

"Good! Her dehydration isn't as bad, so I can start giving her real food today."

"That's great, Nell." Mom sat next to me while I fed Mantha and then helped her go to the bathroom. It really didn't look that hard—or disgusting.

"Now, don't forget what else you have to do today." Mom got up to leave.

Since we're homeschooled, Mom and Dad give us our schoolwork. We do some kind of lessons all year around—but not necessarily sitting at a desk. There are days when we have assignments and Mom or Dad instructs us, similar to what kids do in school. But other times we go out for the whole day, like to a museum or historical site or to volunteer in the community. I've figured out that Mom and Dad like it best when we learn things without ever noticing that we're being taught.

Some of our work is independent study, with our parents supervising but letting us follow our own interests and ideas. I usually choose between the piano and my computer, which I use to write (mostly in my journal), research, and even compose songs using a program I got for Christmas.

Charley loves to draw, and while spelling just comes naturally to him, he actually likes to read the dictionary. He's also amazingly good at geography. He does jigsaw puzzles of maps, and he even likes to bite his sandwiches into shapes and have Jack and I guess which state or country they are. Charley gets this from our dad, who is a travel agent. Dad reads atlases the way other people read novels.

Dad likes to tell a story about the time he was quizzing Jack and me about countries in Africa. "What is the capital of Ethiopia?" he asked.

When neither Jack nor I knew the answer, three-year-old Charley pulled his thumb out of his mouth and said, "Addis Ababa." Dad freaked out! "What country is Addis Ababa the capital of?" he asked. "Eepeeopeeuh!" Charley yelled. He's been Dad's star geography student ever since.

Jack is like Dad in that he never sits still, and they both love being outside. When Jack has to be in the house, he likes to build stuff—Legos and models. Jack is smart at math, too, and can figure out problems in his head. He gets that from Mom.

We're in a "real" classroom only one week a year. When the schools give achievement tests, Mom makes arrangements for us to take them with the other kids. At first, I felt kind of awkward on those days, but now that I know all the other kids—and they know me—it's fun. Sure, I feel different. But good different, not weird.

Kids always ask me questions about homeschooling, especially about what I do all day. Some of them wish their parents would let them homeschool, too. Others say they would hate it—like Greta. She likes to have people around all the time; she can't understand how I don't get bored when I'm alone. She thinks I should ask to go to school again, to try it out, even just for a year. Someday I might, but for now I'm happy. I get to do a lot of things that I really want to do. Like waking up that morning and feeding a baby squirrel instead of walking to the bus stop in the rain, which I saw Greta doing.

Since we would be staying home for a while with Mantha, Mom said we'd have more drills and worksheets and written assignments than usual. I wondered if that was a test to see if we liked having the squirrel around enough to do more typical schoolwork. I promised myself to act enthusiastic, whether I liked the work or not, and even do *more* than Mom asked for.

We started on schoolwork right after breakfast. First, Mom taught me about prime numbers and factoring. Then I helped Charley while Mom worked with Jack. When it was Charley's turn with Mom, I did three pages of workbook problems and drilled Jack on "mental math," which is what Dad calls the problem-solving Jack does without paper.

Next, I reviewed a long list of spelling words and wrote sentences using them. I made a note to see if Charley could spell *rhinoceros*. Then I finished reading *Tuck Everlasting*. I thought it was a great book and wrote some of my thoughts about it in my journal, which is in a password-protected area on my computer.

I'd been researching Civil War sites in Ohio and nearby states for a family vacation, so I went online to do a little more checking. I printed out a map and made a few notes, but I'd lost interest in the trip. I figured it would have to wait now that we had Mantha.

I kept checking my e-mail for a message from Libby, but there was nothing all morning.

After lunch, I fed Mantha, then I folded and put away two baskets of laundry and straightened my room. I would usually spend an afternoon at home playing the piano, but today I had other things on my mind, so I practiced for only an hour.

I finally got a message from Libby. Before I read it, I made a silent wish that she would volunteer to help me.

Hi Nell,

I was so glad to get your e-mail. I love squirrels, and it does my heart good to hear of one being rescued. But I have to warn you about tackling this project by yourself. This isn't a job for just anyone. You didn't mention where you live, but in many states there are laws against this. You also didn't say how old you are, but I got the impression that you are young. Raising a baby squirrel is a lot of responsibility. I think it would be best for you to find another alternative. Would you like me to speak with your parents?

If you cannot find better arrangements, I will do my best to instruct you. But I am not a licensed wildlife rehabilitator, and you really are supposed to take the squirrel to one. I do understand your circumstances, though, with living out in the country. So, tell me what condition the squirrel is in and how things are going.

And try not to handle the animal too much—only when absolutely necessary. It is not good for either of you to form an attachment.

Best wishes,

Libby

What did she mean "laws against this"? Against what? I was only taking care of a squirrel from my yard—one that needed help just to survive. What could be wrong with that? And Libby didn't say *all* states. Maybe whatever she was talking about was okay in Ohio. Besides, Libby said that *she* raised squirrels. If she did it and she wasn't a licensed rehabilitator, why couldn't I?

I hit *reply* and began to write:

Dear Libby,

Thanks for your response. Don't worry, because actually I'm not that young. I'm 16 years old.

That didn't make any sense. If I were sixteen, couldn't I just drive to wherever I needed to go to find a wildlife rehabilitator? But also, why couldn't my parents drive me? Could I really live so far away that I couldn't get to a town or city without too much trouble? I had to come up with just the right story.

I tried again:

Dear Libby,

Thanks for your response. I am 15 years old, and I think I can handle the responsibility. I'm sorry to say that my parents are not as interested in this animal as I am. They don't think it's worth the price of the gas it would take to drive to a rehabilitator.

The squirrel seems to be in good health. There are no signs of injury or insects. There was dehydration when I first examined her, but she is doing better now.

Since we live so far out in the country, I am homeschooled. So I am able to feed and take care of the baby day or night. I will not handle it too much. I want very much to help this squirrel.

Thank you,

Nell

P.S. I named the squirrel Samantha, but I sometimes call her Mantha.

I hoped that covered everything. I hated making my parents sound so coldhearted, but I really wanted to keep Mantha and I needed Libby's help. What else could I do?

It was mid-afternoon when I made the baby formula for Mantha. She gobbled it up.

Mom came in and sat on the floor next to me.

"Can you show me what you do to make Mantha go to the bathroom?" I asked her.

"Really? You're ready for that?"

"I think so." I wanted Mom to see how mature and responsible I could be.

"Like this." She demonstrated. "See? You try."

I actually made the baby pee! I was more surprised than grossed out, but I must have been making quite a face because Mom got a good laugh from it.

"Be glad it's a very small animal!"

I scrubbed my hands twice and was refilling the hot-water bottle when Charley came running in from the yard.

"Mom! Mom!" He sounded very upset or very excited. I couldn't tell which.

Even Jack came to see what was up.

"What is it?" asked Mom.

"I was playing on the tire swing," Charley said, his words tumbling together, "when another baby squirrel fell out of the tree. It just missed me. Hurry! Come see!"

SIX

We all followed Charley out the back door. Sure enough, in almost the exact spot where Mantha had been the day before was another baby squirrel.

"It's raining squirrels!" Charley squealed.

"Man! I don't believe this," Jack said. "Can we keep 'em both?"

"Don't say 'keep.' We're not *keeping* anything," Mom reminded us.

This baby didn't seem as strong as Mantha. We'd heard Mantha's cries—even though they were faint—from upstairs, and she'd been squirming all around. This one wasn't making any noise at all and was barely moving.

It had to be Mantha's brother or sister. After all, how many squirrel nests could there be in one tree? We still hadn't been able to spot one.

"What does a squirrel nest look like?" asked Charley.

Mom pointed out a big mound of leaves in our neighbor's tree. But there was nothing like that in our ash tree. "They also might build in hollow places—like inside the trunk."

"I told you so," Jack said.

When we looked really hard, we thought we could see a small hole in the trunk at about the same height as our attic window—quite a distance to fall!

"Do you think there are any more babies up there?" Charley asked.

"Hard to say," Mom answered. "I hope not. But since we don't have a ladder that would reach that high, I guess we'll just have to wait to see what happens. Now, we'd better get this little guy into the house and warm him up. By the looks of him, I don't think the mother has come back."

"What do you think happened to the mom?" Charley asked as we walked to the house.

"I'm afraid she may have been hit by a car or one of the neighborhood dogs caught her."

"I bet it was Humphrey," Jack said, referring to a golden retriever that lives on our block. "He chases squirrels all the time."

"Could be," Mom said. "The babies were probably searching for their mother's warmth or her milk when they accidentally fell from the nest."

"It's a good thing they have us now," Charley said.

Back in the kitchen, I carefully checked over the new squirrel. I put the rubber gloves on—to be extra safe—before examining him, although I had read on Libby's Web site that squirrels generally do not carry rabies or any other disease that humans can catch. This would especially be true of tiny babies that had never left their nest. I had stopped wearing the gloves when I fed Mantha, but I always made sure to wash my hands before and after touching her.

Except for a small scratch, there were no major injuries on the new squirrel, but it was even more dehydrated than Mantha had been.

I heated up some Pedialyte while Mom cleaned the scratch

with peroxide. "This one is a boy," she said as she dabbed on some antibiotic cream.

"What should we call him?" Charley asked.

"In *Redwall*, Sam's mother's name is Jess," I said. "So why don't we name him that? It can be a boy's name, too."

"That's pretty good," said Jack.

"I like it," said Charley.

I placed Jess in the drawer to warm up before I tried to feed him. "You have company, Mantha," I said.

I sent an e-mail to Libby, telling her the news.

When I returned, the babies were curled together in a tight circle. They seemed to belong together.

"It's great we have two," I told the boys. "Libby's Web site says it's important for a squirrel to grow up with other squirrels. Now Mantha and Jess have each other."

Greta was excited to meet Jess when she stopped by with her camera after school. Greta loves photography and had an idea for a project: she would take shots that show how a baby squirrel changes as it grows.

"Can I have one of the squirrels, Nell? Please?" she begged.

"They have to be fed every few hours, and you're at school all day."

She had to agree that wouldn't work very well. "When it's old enough to care for itself, can I have one?"

"Here, let's feed them," I said, trying to change the subject. Greta can be very determined. I didn't want to argue with her, but I already couldn't imagine separating my squirrels.

Greta fed formula to Mantha, while I gave Jess some Pedialyte. His dehydration was getting better.

"Mantha ate a lot," said Greta.

"But look, half her food is down the front of her. That always happens. We need to invent a little squirrel bib," I said as I got some damp cotton balls to clean her off.

"Let me get a picture of you with the squirrels." Greta took out her camera. She tucked her short, silky blonde hair behind her ears and looked through the viewfinder. "Everybody, smile!"

I held the babies under my chin and grinned.

We looked at the picture on the camera. It was a close-up. My long, curly, black hair was thrown behind my shoulders, and you could see the weird—at least, I think it's weird—color of my eyes. They're dark green with light golden rings around the pupils. My left eye has a black dot near the bottom of the iris, like a second, smaller pupil that got misplaced. You could count the freckles scattered across my nose. I looked so happy with those tiny creatures cupped to my face. I *was* happy.

Libby wrote back and gave me a warning about feedings:

> An eyedropper is okay for emergencies, but the babies need something they can suck on. Plus, you could accidentally squeeze too hard and force fluid into the babies' lungs and cause pneumonia. If you ever notice one of their noses running—which could still happen when you use a bottle—lay the squirrel with its head downward and gently wipe off its nose.

> At the pet store, you can buy nursing bottles that are used for kittens and puppies. You need the smallest one with the smallest hole in the nipple.

I showed Mom the e-mail, and we went to the pet store for a bottle. From then on, Mom and Dad wouldn't let the boys feed the squirrels. It was all up to me. I was very careful.

The end of the one-week trial period came and went. Even Dad didn't have any complaints about the way things were going. We kept the squirrels' drawer clean (no smells), and I never missed a feeding. Now that I knew how to make the squirrels go to the bathroom, Mom didn't have to get up at night, although she sometimes did. Jack and Charley took turns getting up with me, too.

Libby wrote to me frequently. One time she said:

> I'm still not sure this is the best thing. Maybe I could talk your parents into taking the squirrels to a professional.

I was doing a good job, I thought. Why did she have to keep bringing up professionals?

I wrote:

> I think it's just best if we don't talk about the squirrels to my parents.

At the same time that I was trying to keep Libby from talking to my parents, they wanted to know more about the grown-up I was writing to online.

"You said you wanted this to be my project," I complained when they asked to see printouts of her e-mails.

"Of course, Nell," Mom said, "but that won't keep us from

being sure that you're safe. Plus, I want to make sure that you understand the instructions Libby gives you."

My parents regularly asked questions about Libby, and I liked finding out the answers. For example, Libby wrote that she was twenty-four years old and had graduated from college with a degree in journalism.

> I got interested in wildlife when I was thirteen and found a baby squirrel, just the way you found Mantha and Jess. My parents let me keep it—we lived in Florida, where it was legal. I got a book at the library and tried to take care of the squirrel on my own. It died after about a month.

> A couple years later, a friend found a baby squirrel in her yard, and I took care of it. That one lived, and I released it. I raised and released four other baby squirrels (two at a time) before I went away to college. I haven't had a squirrel since, but I am still a big fan! That's why I started the Web site about a year ago.

Libby also wanted to know more about me. She asked if I lived on a farm and about homeschooling. I told her a little about homeschooling, which was easy to do, but mostly I avoided talking about myself. I found that if I asked her a lot of questions, it kept her from asking about me.

I hated the lying, but I was just trying to make things work. Besides, I couldn't imagine that anyone could take better care of the squirrels than I did. After all, I loved them.

SEVEN

"Is there something shiny on that one's face?" Greta asked. "I thought I saw something."

"Which one?" I asked.

"That one." She pointed at Mantha. The squirrels were about five weeks old, but Greta still couldn't tell them apart.

I picked up Mantha and saw a twinkle of light.

"Her eyes are opening!" I said. I was so excited that the squirrels would finally be able to see me. "This is great! Libby says that after their eyes open, the squirrels' chances of surviving are much better."

That was the good news. I didn't tell anyone the "bad" news: Libby also told me that when their eyes opened, they'd be able to start learning to take care of themselves. Of course, I wanted to know the squirrels would be okay. But I didn't want to think about what would happen when they could care for themselves.

The next day, Jess's eyes opened, too.

Changes came faster and faster. The babies still slept a lot, but when they were awake, they were getting to be a handful.

I couldn't imagine a mother squirrel taking care of such active babies in a small nest on a tree limb. (I'd read that squirrel litters could be four babies and sometimes even more.) Feeding time was especially crazy. The nursing bottle I bought at the pet store made things a little easier, but Libby had another warning:

> There are a lot of things that can go wrong with feeding the squirrels. They probably won't stop eating just because they're full. If they overeat, it could cause bloating or diarrhea. Tell me immediately if this happens! Take extra care to measure how much you give them. I'm attaching a chart that tells exactly how much they should get based on their age.

Since I was the one to feed both of them, I had a lot to juggle. If I was lucky, I could feed one while the other one slept. But they had already figured out that when I came into the room, it was time to eat. As soon as they heard the bathroom door open or the light went on, they got excited and started climbing on top of each other, like it was a contest to see which one could get to me first. The commotion didn't stop until the meal was over.

I tried letting one run up and down my shirt and pants for exercise while I fed the other, but this didn't work if I tried to feed Jess first. Mantha refused to wait her turn. She'd run down my arm and try to grab the bottle away. It was hopeless to make her go second. Jess didn't mind, though. He'd sit on my shoulder and stick his nose in my ear, tickling me with little snooting sounds while I fed Mantha.

After eating, the babies would curl up on my lap. I'd stroke their sides while they napped. I could sit there for an hour, too happy to move. I've heard people say that only cats purr, but I know, sure as anything, that Mantha and Jess purred during those times.

Another big change that came once their eyes opened was that the squirrels didn't need help going to the bathroom anymore. I had looked forward to this, but it turned out to be a new problem. When I helped them to go, their nest stayed clean. Now it was terrible. The boys and I had to clean out their drawer many times a day. We switched to shredded newspapers instead of the flannel nightgown or other rags because of the stinky laundry. I knew I had to be careful or Dad would complain.

When the babies were about six weeks old, Libby wrote:

> Mantha and Jess are ready to start feeding themselves. Squirrels don't just lean over their food like a dog or cat. They have bendable toes that let them grasp things, so they eat more like humans, holding their food in their front paws. It may take a couple of days before they can balance on their back feet without toppling over. But with practice, they'll soon be feeding themselves nuts and sunflower seeds and bits of fruits and vegetables.
>
> Be careful with introducing new foods, though. Never give them more than one new food at a time, and wait a couple of days before trying another one or it may cause diarrhea.

Libby told me that squirrels have "rodent teeth," which means their front teeth grow continuously throughout their lives—at a rate of six inches a year! This balances out all the wear and tear that comes from opening those hard nutshells.

> Now that their teeth are coming in, Mantha and Jess need to chew on things—to keep their teeth filed down, like you do with your fingernails—or their teeth could grow so long they won't be able to eat.

Jack and Charley gathered sticks and pinecones in the yard, and the squirrels knew what to do with them right away. You could hear them gnawing from the kitchen.

One morning toward the end of April, I went into the bathroom for their first feeding of the day, and the squirrels weren't in their drawer! I couldn't imagine how they disappeared. It was a small room without many places to hide, and we always kept the door closed so Dotty and Murphy couldn't get at them. I was starting to panic when they popped out from the space between their drawer and the wall.

"How did you two get out?" I asked them.

I put them back in the drawer, and they quickly revealed how they'd made their escape: Mantha crawled up on top of the hot-water bottle, put her front paws against the edge of the drawer, and flipped headfirst over the side. Jess was right behind her. I scooped them both up.

"You two boogers!"

I showed Mom what they'd been up to.

"We can start by taking out the 'ladder,'" she said. "They don't need the bottle to help them stay warm anymore."

"I know," I said. "But they'd still be snuggling up against a warm mother at night if they could." And I knew that they still curled up against the bottle.

"You're going to have to find something else to keep them in, Nell," Mom went on. "Before long, they'll be able to climb out—even without the bottle. And it's not safe for them to be wandering around without someone watching them. There's not much in here, but they could still find a way to get into trouble."

We went to the pet store to find a better nest for the squirrels.

"This one is so awesome," Jack said, whistling out the S sounds. He pointed to a cage meant for a very large dog. "It would give them more room to play in."

"I think they could crawl out between the bars," Charley said, and he was right.

"And that size is too big for our little bathroom," Mom added. "Do you want to move them to the basement? That would probably make your dad happy. He would like it if we could use that bathroom again."

"No!" I protested. "It's dark and damp in the basement. I don't want the babies down there."

"How about this?" Charley asked, pointing to a cat carrier.

"It would be easy to move around and wouldn't take up much room," Mom said.

"Plus, it kind of looks like a drey," I said. A *drey* is a squirrel's leafy nest. The carrier was brown—the color of the dead leaves you see in a drey—and enclosed all around with hard plastic. There was a metal grate on the door so they wouldn't be able to chew their way out.

"Works for me," Mom said. She had agreed to pay for half of the cost. The boys and I split the rest from our allowances.

We couldn't wait to show the squirrels their new nest. I put the carrier in the bathroom and took the squirrels out of their old drawer. I opened the door to the carrier, and they ran right in to explore. Charley found their old flannel nightgown in a box of rags in the basement and put it in with them so the nest would feel familiar. They immediately started to paw at the material. It reminded me of a couple arranging the furniture in their new home.

But I knew this was only temporary. Mantha and Jess couldn't live in the bathroom forever. I had to come up with another idea, or they would soon be living in the basement—or worse.

EIGHT

My life had become centered on the squirrels—which I loved—but there were other things going on in Meadowlake.

For one thing, in early May, baseball season began. Not that I like baseball; I hate baseball. In fact, I'm not crazy about any sport. First, I'm not very athletic. I'm tall and skinny, and while I don't know of any scientific studies on this, I think my feet are too big for running and jumping and stuff like that. My dad teases me that when I turn sideways, all you see are my feet. I just feel awkward playing sports. Give me a computer or piano any day.

But Jack is a natural athlete. Mom said he was climbing before he crawled, and he was walking by the time he was nine months old. Today, he never walks if he can run. And he loves to throw and catch and jump and . . . you name it. Jack is especially obsessed with baseball. His head is filled with the names of teams and players and all kinds of numbers and statistics. His room, which he shares with poor Charley, is packed with tons of baseball junk—balls, hats, gloves, books, banners. Some are even autographed. And he has two enormous boxes of baseball cards that are all categorized. It started out as an assignment from Dad to put things in alphabetical order. Then Dad had Jack sort the teams by geographical regions. Now the collection has grown into a huge project with an organization that only Jack understands. He won't let anyone touch the cards in case one might be put back in the wrong place or get a fingerprint on it.

Even though Jack thinks about baseball all year 'round, spring is special. As soon as spring training starts, he follows every move made by his favorite team, the Cleveland Indians. And he turns our backyard into a mini-training camp while he waits for his Little League team to begin practicing.

Jack is catcher for the Bearcats. He has never missed a game since his first T-ball at-bat when he was five years old. That's a lot of games. And my parents have made me go to every one of them. There are a million things I'd rather do—clean my room, give the dog a bath, watch a golf tournament on TV, catch a cold. *Anything* else!

Baseball season stretched ahead of me like an eternity.

Whenever possible, I talk Greta into coming to the games with me. I was glad when she agreed to go to the first game of the season.

Sometimes Joey Rafferty, the coach's son, comes to the games, too. He's a year older than I am, and his brother is on the team with Jack. I like it when Joey is there because it gives me someone to talk to. Unfortunately, Joey plays on another team, so he often has games of his own at the same time. He made it to this one, though. Just before the game started, I saw him walking across the outfield with another boy.

"This is Russ Cason," Joey said as they sat in the grass next to me and Greta. "His family moved here from Michigan. They live in the Woodruffs' old house on Sheffield."

"Hi, I'm Greta. I see you leaving Belzer's homeroom when I'm going in for math," Greta said to Russ.

"I thought you looked familiar," he said.

"Nell's homeschooled," Joey told him.

"Don't you live on Chambers Avenue, near Dalton Street?" Russ asked me. "I bike past there on my way to my uncle's house. I've seen you and your brothers in the yard."

"Yes," I said. I wondered what we were doing when he saw us.

I couldn't help but notice Russ's eyes. They're the color of a blueberry Popsicle, which is kind of surprising because he isn't blond or a freckle-faced redhead like Joey. Russ has black hair and olive skin.

"Go, Bearcats!" one of the mothers yelled as the team took the field.

"It's a silly name," I said. "What kind of animal is a bearcat, anyway?"

"It's probably some mutant life-form." Joey laughed. "That makes it the perfect name for these guys."

"That's mean!" Greta said, but we both giggled.

"Actually, *bearcat* is another name for the red panda," said Russ. "It looks like a raccoon and lives in the Himalayas."

We all turned to stare at him.

"What can I say?" Russ shrugged his shoulders. "I live with two science teachers. My dad teaches geology at the community college, and Mom is the earth sciences teacher at the high school."

"I should have warned you," Joey said. "Russ knows everything about animals."

"Nell has baby squirrels," Greta jumped in. She has a major crush on Joey, so I knew she was just showing off, but I didn't want everyone to know about the squirrels. The more people who knew, the bigger the chance that someone would take them away from me.

"Russ *hunts* squirrels," Joey said.

I was stunned. "You do?"

"I hunt with my dad and granddad, but not for squirrels," Russ said matter-of-factly. "What kind of squirrels do you have? Eastern grays?"

I nodded and turned away. "Go, Bearcats!" I yelled, pretending to care about a play at first base. I didn't think I was going to like this new guy, blue eyes or not. I've always hated the idea of hunting, and now that I had the squirrels, I hated it even more. Russ seemed totally fine with it.

"A full-grown squirrel can bite through a finger bone," Russ said, not taking the hint that I didn't want to talk with him anymore. "Socializing them with humans can be bad news. You do plan to release them, don't you?"

I knew I wasn't going to like this guy.

NINE

"Can we take the squirrels into the living room so we can all watch them?" Charley asked. The half-bath offered a pretty cramped play area.

"I guess we could give it a try," Mom said. "Let's see where Dotty and Murphy are so they can't walk in on us."

"Man! What do you think they'll do?" Jack asked. "Lick the squirrels to death?"

"They wouldn't hurt *anything*," added Charley.

"No, I don't think they would, either," Mom said.

"Then why do we have to keep them away from the squirrels?" Jack asked. "It might be funny to see what they do together."

"Think about this—" Mom said. "If the squirrels learn to trust Dotty and Murphy, they might trust any dog or cat. Would you want them to trust Humphrey or Wendell?"

"No way!" Charley said.

"Exactly," said Mom.

When we were sure our pets were locked safely away in the kitchen, I went to get Mantha and Jess. I sat on the floor in the bathroom and opened the door to the carrier. As usual, they quickly ran up onto my shoulders. I got up and went into the living room. The babies weren't used to traveling like this—they had rarely been out of the bathroom—and they dug their claws into my shoulders as I walked.

I sat in the middle of the room. After a minute or two, Mantha crawled down to the floor. She began to walk around, slowly at first. Soon Jess joined her. Gradually, they became more adventurous. They ran one way, then the other, like they couldn't make up their minds what to do next.

"Maybe the babies would enjoy a little musical entertainment." I sat at the piano. As soon as I started to play, Jess ran up my pants leg, down my sleeve, and onto the piano. I put him on my shoulder and played a sonatina that has lots of fast scales going up and down. Jess sat watching with his head moving back and forth, back and forth. Finally, he ran down my sleeve and pounced on one of my hands, like a kitten on a ball of string.

On the other side of the room, Mantha quickly got herself into trouble. She climbed up the back of an overstuffed chair and leaped onto the bookshelves. We were all amazed because we'd never seen her jump before. The thrill ended when she hopped up onto some books and peed.

"Man!" said Jack.

"Uh-oh," said Charley.

There was no *good* place in the room for her to pee, but this was maybe the worst. Mom treasures her books. I hurried over to let Mantha climb onto my shoulder.

"I wonder if it's possible to litter-train a squirrel," Mom grumbled as she cleaned up the mess.

"Don't even think about it," said Dad, who had just come into the room. "We want them outside as soon as possible."

Dad was losing patience with the squirrels. He said they were taking up too much of our time—especially mine—and he was getting annoyed with them living in the bathroom, even though we had another, much bigger one we used. And no matter what I did, there was starting to be a smell. Dad said our house was "taking on the distinctive stench of a petting zoo." Plus, both Dad and Mom were tired of not being able to go on trips. They were itching to get away from the house and on the road.

I didn't mind the smells or staying home or anything else about the squirrels. I didn't even mind that I was the one who took care of them the most. Me! The same person who complained when I had to walk Dotty or clean Murphy's litter box or the hamster cage. The squirrels were special. They made *me* feel special.

TEN

$\mathcal{L}ibby$ $said$ $that$ $baby$ $squirrels$ are usually weaned from their mother's milk and living completely on their own by ten to twelve weeks old. But for human-raised squirrels, it's better to wait until they're a little older—fourteen weeks—to release them. To prepare for that, when the babies were about nine weeks old, Libby wrote that they needed to start experiencing outdoor life.

> This is the age when baby squirrels in the wild would start adventuring away from their mother. Take them outside and let them practice climbing on trees. They need to get the feel of the outdoors.

If I did have to release the squirrels one day, I wanted them to be ready, but I hated the thought of taking them outside. I was afraid they might get away, and I'd never get them back.

Then I got the idea to move Mantha and Jess to the screened porch. It would get them out of the bathroom, and they could have the sights, sounds, and smells of the outdoors. But they couldn't run off, and other animals couldn't get at them. And the porch was in the back of the house, so people wouldn't see them, either.

Charley and Jack found a big tree limb in the nearby ravine and dragged it home. We broke off the smaller branches that were sticking out of it and propped it up in a corner of the porch. The squirrels got lots of practice climbing all the way from the floor to the ceiling.

Now the squirrels were on the porch all day long, and the boys and I were with them as much as Mom and Dad would allow.

"I can get much better pictures out here," Greta said when we showed her the new arrangement. "Tons of my photos so far have at least part of your toilet in them."

I turned to the squirrel sitting high on the branch in the corner. "Did you hear that, Jess? Greta doesn't like the way you decorated your room."

"How do you know that's Jess from over here?"

"It's easy to tell them apart," I said. "Jess has tufts of fur that stand up behind his ears. He's kind of scruffy looking, and Mantha is sleek and shiny."

"And Mantha's feet look different," Jack added. "There are more colors. Her feet are red and gray and brown, all swirled together. Jess's are just gray."

"They act different, too," Charley said. "Jess is much nicer. Mantha is kind of pushy."

"Really?" Greta asked. "I never noticed that."

"It's true!" I laughed. "Jess is a lot sweeter than Mantha. And calmer, too."

Mantha was just plain stubborn. She'd never give up on anything—from being the first one at the food to claiming the spot on my right shoulder, which for some reason both squirrels preferred to my left one. If Jess got there first, Mantha might start a fight. I learned the hard way to keep my hair pulled up when I was on the porch—at least in a ponytail, but a bun or tucked under a hat was even better—so the squirrels wouldn't get tangled up in it.

We kept the cat carrier on the porch with them. Sometimes, Jess liked to add to their "nest." I noticed him gathering materials—once he pulled out strands of my hair!—and taking them into the carrier. I brought him other stuff, such as dryer lint, yarn, or pieces of fabric. As soon as I'd put something down, Jess would grab it up and carry it inside the carrier and find a place for it.

"Have you added anything new to your life list lately?" Greta asked, picking up a notebook from the stack of my schoolwork.

"Yeah, a few," I said.

A life list is a book you keep for bird-watching. Last fall, Mom got me a field guide and a CD of birdcalls. She hoped that I would enjoy being outside more. I began keeping track of the birds I saw in a notebook that I take with me everywhere—on vacations or day trips, to the library and Jack's ball games, and even to my piano lessons, in case I have to wait for Mom to pick me up. I also took it on the porch with me every day when I went out with the squirrels.

Greta was looking over my list when Mantha decided to climb onto her shoulder. On the way up, she left a scratch on Greta's arm. "Yow!" Greta squealed. The scream frightened Mantha, and she left another scratch—a bigger one—on the way down.

Jack couldn't resist scolding Greta. "You're supposed to wear long-sleeve shirts," he said, his tooth whistling. "If Mom had seen you, she never would have let you past her."

Mom was really strict about this rule. Squirrels' claws are razor-sharp, and scratches—squirrel tracks, I call them—are one of the nastier problems that come from living with squirrels. Mom was in a constant battle against squirrel tracks.

"I forgot," Greta said, looking at her arm. "But I won't do that again."

"I'll get something to clean you up," I said.

I knew the routine well. Even when we wore long sleeves and pants, the boys and I still occasionally got squirrel tracks. Mom set up a first-aid station in the kitchen and kept it supplied.

After I cleaned Greta's arm, I tried to distract her from thinking about the scratches. When we first found the squirrels, Greta would stop by every day to see them. But the excitement kind of wore off for her. She still liked them, but mostly she would rather do other things—go somewhere—when we were together. If the squirrel tracks were a reason she wasn't as thrilled about her visits anymore, I wanted to remind her about the good things, too.

"Come on. Let's look in the yard for some new props for your models. Then you can take pictures."

"Ahhh, the glamorous life of a photographer," Greta said as we carefully closed the door behind us so Mantha and Jess couldn't follow us out.

We searched the backyard for anything the squirrels might like to gnaw on—sticks, acorns, pinecones—then moved on to the side and front yards.

"Lose something?"

I looked up and saw Russ Cason put his foot on the curb, bringing his bike to a stop in front of my house.

"Hi," Greta said. "No, we're just looking for some sticks for the squirrels to chew on."

"I'm in a hurry today, but I'd really like to see them sometime," Russ said.

I didn't say anything.

"Oh, sure," Greta said. "Whenever you want."

"Great!" Russ pushed off from the curb. "See you later."

"Why did you tell him that?" I asked Greta as soon as he was out of earshot.

"Why not? He might bring Joey, too."

Was that all she cared about? If Joey came over? What about the squirrels?

"Don't you remember? Russ is a hunter."

"Nell! What are you thinking? He won't hunt Mantha and Jess."

"I know that, but I still don't want him around my squirrels. How could he like animals and *shoot* them? I just wish you hadn't invited him over."

"Sorry. But he's really nice, and he knows a lot about animals. You should talk to him more."

Yeah, that'll happen, I thought.

After Greta left, I fixed some food for the squirrels with a little applesauce in it. I still gave the squirrels a bottle at night even though they were eating on their own. Maybe it was more for me than it was for them.

At sundown, I put them into the cat carrier and took them back to their old spot in the bathroom.

"Good night, babies," I whispered and switched off the light. They responded with little grunting sounds as they settled in to sleep.

Dad turned on the kitchen light. "I thought they lived on the porch now."

"I like them inside at night," I said.

"Nell," he said, "I'm so proud of the way you've taken care of them. That is a big accomplishment! But I'm afraid you are too attached. I'd like to talk with Libby about the timing of the release and how to handle it."

I couldn't let that happen! I tried to think quickly. "She told me they'd be ready at fourteen weeks. I'm getting them ready. A little at a time."

"Good. I want to see things moving ahead."

"As soon as it's warm enough, I'll leave them on the porch at night. Don't worry. I have a plan."

Or I would. Tomorrow.

ELEVEN

Mantha and Jess didn't live alone on the porch. The Daves lived there, too. The Daves were moths. Promethea moths, to be exact. At least they were going to be. They had been in their cocoons since the fall and wouldn't emerge until about July.

Promethea are large, beautiful moths that might even be mistaken for butterflies. Mom's friend Ann gave the moths to us as eggs the summer before. Ann raises moths and butterflies as a hobby, and has different kinds of eggs and larvae, which is another word for caterpillars. She gave us ten of the teensy eggs stuck on a piece of paper inside a plastic sandwich bag, along with instructions on how to care for them.

"Don't expect all of them to hatch," Ann told us. "But you might get five or six caterpillars."

We examined the eggs with a magnifying glass every day last summer until we saw tiny caterpillars—eight of them!—coming out. Then we were responsible for feeding them. We got permission to take a couple of leaves from a sweet-gum tree in the yard of our next-door neighbor, Mrs. Brumley, and put them in their bag. Ann said only specific types of leaves would do, depending on the type of caterpillar. Each day, we'd empty out their poop and put in fresh leaves. Next, one of us would breathe into the bag. The moisture from our breath gave the caterpillars the water they needed.

"We should name them," Charley had said.

"They all look alike, Charley," I replied. "How would we ever tell them apart?"

"Maybe we could give them all the same name," Jack had suggested. "You know, like in that Dr. Seuss story called 'Too Many Daves,' about Mrs. McCave who 'had twenty-three sons, and she named them all Dave.'"

This seemed like the perfect answer. The caterpillars became the Daves.

The Daves had been pale green with a slightly bluish tint. They had four reddish-orange spikes near their heads and a yellowish one near their rears, plus some other black or blue spots in each of their body segments. As they grew, the Daves would periodically shed their skins, and it seemed they had brighter, more beautiful colors each time.

When they outgrew their bag, we moved the Daves into one of those large, clear plastic jugs that dog food comes in. If we opened the lid, we could actually hear them munching on their leaves.

Caterpillars are eating machines. In its first two weeks, a monarch butterfly caterpillar grows to 2,700 times its size at birth; if a human baby grew at that rate, a six-pound newborn would weigh more than eight tons—16,200 pounds—by the time it was two weeks old! The Daves were practically microscopic size when they hatched, and they grew to be as big as my index finger, but even fatter.

One day in early autumn, I had noticed the first silver threads of a cocoon covering part of a leaf. I held the leaf in my hand, and we watched as the Dave repeatedly moved his head back and forth, strengthening and adding to his work. Then the Dave pulled his head and rear sections in opposite directions, causing the leaf to roll up around him, and he started moving his head out beyond the edge of the leaf.

"He's looking for something to anchor the cocoon to," explained Ann, who Mom had invited to watch with us. "Put a stick next to him."

I placed the Dave on the floor with a large twig nearby, and sure enough, it was pulled into the effort. This was really a great plan of nature's, Ann said. "If the Dave were making the cocoon in a tree, and the leaf fell to the ground, he might be stepped on or eaten. Attaching the cocoon to a small branch is a pretty smart way to stay safe."

Within a couple of days, all eight of the Daves were wrapped up in their cocoons. We kept the jug on the porch, but left the lid off so they could fly free once they came out.

We had spent weeks with the Daves, studying them every day. But by the time the squirrels moved onto the porch, the Daves had been in their cocoons for months. We hadn't really thought about them much lately. Until I came out to the porch one spring day and found Mantha chewing away on a cocoon. I was horrified.

"MOM!!!" I screamed. "HELP! HELP!!!"

She came running out to the porch. Jack and Charley were right behind her.

"Mantha is eating one of the Daves!" I shrieked.

Mantha, frightened by my screaming, dropped the Dave and scrambled up the branch in the corner of the porch, where Jess was already trying to get away from me.

Mom placed one hand over her heart. "Nell," she said,

putting her other hand on the doorjamb for support, "you scared me half to death!"

"But Mom," I said, "the Dave!"

We looked to where Mantha had dropped him. About a third of the cocoon had been eaten away, and the rest of it was writhing back and forth. It reminded me of a cobra swaying to a snake-charmer's flute. We all stood frozen in place until the movement came to a stop.

"It's dead," Jack said quietly.

We looked up at Mantha, who was grooming her tail, no longer frightened and not bothered at all by what had happened.

"We can't blame her for following her instincts." Mom sighed. "I just didn't know squirrels ate things like that."

I didn't know it, either, but I felt guilty about leaving the Daves in danger.

We moved the rest of the cocoons—still in the open plastic jug—to the living room, where they'd be safe from the squirrels. Then, we looked inside the damaged cocoon to see what the Dave had been doing in there. All we saw was wet, dark-brown mush.

"What is that stuff?" I asked. "What happened to the caterpillar?"

Mom drove us to Ann's house to find out.

"What you're seeing," she told us, "is an earlier stage of metamorphosis. When the caterpillar is inside its cocoon, it releases chemicals that have been stored in its body. These chemicals cause the tissues to dissolve. This mush then somehow reorganizes itself into a completely different body with wings! It's incredible enough to think of a caterpillar becoming a beautiful winged creature, isn't it? But think of this goo knowing exactly how to turn itself into a certain kind of moth or butterfly."

"Now I'm kind of glad Mantha ate the Dave," Jack said as we drove home, "so we could see what was going on in there."

"Well, I'm not glad," I said, "but it *was* interesting."

We buried the rest of the poor Dave in the flower bed outside the screened porch. I thought about how cruel nature can be sometimes—as Mantha had shown us—but, at the same time, how wonderful and amazing.

TWELVE

"Nell, would you play catch with me?" Jack asked.

"I don't feel like it." I was sitting on the porch, writing some notes about the squirrels. I thought maybe someday I'd write a book about them.

"Come on, please? I promise not to throw the ball so high this time."

"Sorry, I already have plans," I said, hoping he wouldn't ask what they were. But avoiding playing ball with Jack was a good enough reason to come up with some things to do.

It was a warm, sunny day, so I decided to take a walk. I told Mom where I was going and headed toward the ravine near our house, where I thought I might see some different kinds of birds. I took along my life list.

As I walked through the deep shadows of the trees, I heard a commotion just off the pathway. There on the ground was a huge bird with a squirrel in its talons. It was the closest I'd ever been to such a big bird, and it was frightening to see. I figured it must be some kind of hawk.

The squirrel was still alive, its chest heaving with rapid breaths.

The bird stopped whatever it was about to do and stared at me. My heart was probably beating as fast as the squirrel's, but I had to help. I shouted and grabbed a stick to scare the bird. It stared at me for a long moment before releasing the squirrel, spreading its huge wingspan, and flying up to a nearby tree.

I stood there, waving the stick and making loud barking sounds, hoping that the squirrel had plenty of time to get away and that the bird wouldn't decide to fly at me.

"The hawk has to eat, too," a voice behind me said. I nearly jumped out of my skin.

Russ grinned at my reaction.

"What are you doing here?" I asked angrily. My face was burning.

"I was fishing in the creek over there when I heard a scream. I thought someone needed help."

"Oh." I couldn't stop blushing.

"You know, the hawk will only find another animal to eat," he said. "That's what they do."

"Yeah, I know," I said, although I hadn't given it a thought. "But I had to . . . It just seemed like . . . I wanted to . . . So, you're fishing?"

Russ nodded, still grinning. I hated that my rescue attempt was amusing to him.

"Want to see?" he asked.

"I guess so," I said, even though fishing seemed a lot like hunting to me. I wanted to show how offended I was, to let him know that I didn't approve of either hunting *or* fishing. But I still felt embarrassed about Russ seeing me barking and threatening a bird, and I couldn't seem to find the right words. So I followed him.

He sat on the bank and picked up the pole. He took an

earthworm from a small can and put it on the hook. Then he flicked his wrist, and the line landed in the deepest part of the water.

"Do you enjoy any activities where animals don't die?" I blurted out.

Russ looked stunned. It was his turn to try to think of something to say.

Suddenly, I could think of a lot of things.

"Can't you just play video games? You could shoot guns without really hurting anything."

"You're joking, right?"

"No," I said.

"I would've thought you'd like that I do stuff outdoors since you like squirrels so much. You're out here hiking instead of sitting in front of a computer, aren't you? I love nature as much as you do."

"How can you say that if you hunt?" But I liked that he called what I was doing "hiking." It sounded adventurous. I wasn't just trying to avoid sports, as usual.

"Hunting *connects* me to nature," Russ said.

"Well, it seems like a bad way to do it."

"It's not!"

"Why should *you* decide when something dies?"

"I'm like that red-tail hawk back there," he said. (Of course, Russ knew exactly what kind of bird it was!) "Do you think he felt sorry for catching that squirrel?"

"That's different. Hawks have to hunt to eat. You don't. How is what you do good?"

"Hunters actually help nature," he said. He was still holding his fishing pole, occasionally giving a gentle tug on the line. I was pacing along the bank behind him.

"You've got to be kidding me," I said.

"I'm serious! Animals can starve to death when there are too many in an area. And some animals damage property and cause health problems—like deer and Canada geese—when there are too many of them. Then they get in trouble with the humans. Hunters help . . . "— he paused—"keep things in balance. At least, responsible hunters do."

"Even if that's true, I don't understand how it could be fun. Killing things, I mean." I leaned against a tree, a little confused. The calmness, even politeness, of his voice had drained the anger right out of me. It no longer seemed like arguing. We were just talking.

"If I do bag something—and my dad and I hunt ducks and geese, not mammals—that's only part of the experience. Like my dad says, they call it a *hunt* not a *kill*. There are other things that make hunting fun."

"What other things?"

"Well, for example, watching nature up close, trying to out-think an animal in its own territory."

"Having a gun seems like a big head start over a poor little duck," I said.

"Not as much as you'd think. You're wearing and carrying heavy gear, trying to walk through mud and water, aiming at something that's moving really fast. A teal can fly sixty miles an hour!"

"And the fun part would be . . . ?"

He laughed. "It *is* fun! Being outside, waiting for that split second of sunrise when the first shots can be fired. Plus, I spend time with my dad and granddad."

"There are other things you can do outdoors with your family." Thinking about Mantha and Jess, I added, "What if it's a mother you kill? A mother with babies waiting for her?"

"When you hunt, you get used to the idea of something dying. I don't feel bad—as long as it's a clean kill. I don't want the animal to suffer."

I shuddered.

"What's that?" He pointed to my notebook—changing the subject, I noticed.

"My life list," I said, ready to explain. But he already knew what I meant.

"You're a bird-watcher?" Russ was quiet for a moment, and he appeared to be listening to something. "There is a red-eyed vireo in the area right now," he said.

"Wow! You really do know a lot about animals." I could tell he'd spent a long time learning about nature. A lot longer than I had.

"Can I look at it?" he asked.

I handed him my list.

"How long have you been keeping this?"

"Eight or nine months, I guess."

"Not bad. Maybe you do understand a little about how I feel when I'm hunting."

I didn't know what he meant, but before I could ask, the end of his fishing pole dipped into the water.

Russ gripped the pole. He gave it a jerk and reeled in a small fish. Then he took the fish from the hook and gently placed it back into the stream.

"No harm," he said. "I always release the fish I catch—unless it's for dinner."

I nodded slowly.

"I really would like to meet your squirrels sometime, Nell. Unarmed," he said with a smile.

THIRTEEN

It was a rainy spring. I didn't mind, though. I didn't need to ride my bike or rollerblade. I was happy to be with my squirrels.

On days when the rain showers were light, I'd sit on the porch with Mantha and Jess. But if the wind blew hard or there was lightning, I'd hurry the babies into their carrier and take them back into the bathroom.

Deep down, I knew it was silly, but I didn't want them outside— even on the screened porch—in bad weather. Still, it made me sad to keep them cooped up after they were used to having a bigger space on the porch, so I'd sit and play with them on the bathroom floor until the storm blew over.

One Saturday afternoon in late May, I was on the porch reading while Mantha and Jess napped on my lap. Dark clouds rolled in, and raindrops tapped at the awning. It was a light rain, but I could feel something stronger coming. Before long, the phone lines started to sway, and I could hear the tire swing hitting against the tree as the wind tossed it about. Thunder rumbled.

"Come on, babies," I said. "Looks like we'd better go inside."

I moved them into the bathroom and opened the door to the carrier. I sat on the floor, and they ran up to my shoulders. If they couldn't climb on their branch, I was the next best thing.

"Nell, telephone!" Dad called from the kitchen.

I put a small mound of Cheerios on the floor and placed the babies next to it. "Here, you guys work on this. I'll be right back."

It was Greta, inviting me to sleep over. We had been talking for only a couple of minutes when I heard a sound from the bathroom.

It was Mom, repeating, "Oh, no. Oh, no." Her voice was low, but I could hear the alarm in it. I dropped the phone and ran to see what was wrong. When I got there, she was reaching into the toilet, which seemed to be filled with black water. My knees went weak as I realized it wasn't dark water but dark *fur* in the water.

One of the squirrels had fallen into the toilet! I could see Mom's hand shaking as she pulled it from the water.

In the dark, wet fur, I saw an eye blink.

Mom grabbed a towel, threw it on the floor, and placed the squirrel onto it. I was moving to help when I realized Mom was reaching back into the water. I hadn't noticed it was still dark.

She pulled out the other squirrel. I searched its face. But there was no blink, no movement. The body was limp.

It felt like the room was spinning around me. I sank to the floor. I had to lie down or I thought I would faint.

"Nell," Mom said softly, "I'm so sorry."

"What happened?" I heard Charley ask from the doorway.

"An accident," Mom said. "It's Jess."

Charley started to cry, and Jack and Dad came to see what was going on. As soon as Dad saw, he put his hands on the boys' shoulders and guided them out of the room.

I felt the cool tile floor against my face and smelled a mixture of wet fur and pine-scented cleaner. I saw Mantha next to me. She was very still, just blinking. I placed my hand on her side. Then I sat up and looked at Jess, lying on a towel next to the door.

A scene from a book or movie seemed more real than those few minutes. One of my worst fears had come true, but it came quietly, almost in slow motion, not at all as I would have imagined. I softly ran my fingers over Jess's wet tail. I pressed the palm of my hand against his paws.

I felt Mom's arm around my shoulder. I could tell from her breath against my hair that she was crying. I folded the ends of the towel over Jess's body.

"Come on, Nell," Mom said. "Let's go to the other room."

Mom picked up Mantha, wrapped in a towel, and carried her into the living room. Mom sat in the rocking chair and held Mantha to her chest. I sat at Mom's feet and put my head on her knee. I couldn't believe this was happening. I had been gone for only a couple of minutes. Why couldn't I have just left the squirrels on the porch?

I looked toward the kitchen and saw Dad carrying a shoe box. I closed my eyes.

"Mom," Charley cried, "why?"

"It was an accident," Mom said.

"But what happened?" Jack asked.

"The babies were probably just playing," she said. "Maybe they were trying to get to the roll of toilet paper. I guess Jess fell in first. With his body underneath her, Mantha could stay high enough to reach up out of the water for air. But poor Jess couldn't breathe."

"It was just a terrible accident," Mom said again, and I knew she was saying it for me to hear.

"I wish there was no such thing as this," Charley said, sobbing, "no such thing as dying."

"I know," Mom said. "It's so sad. It's so hard to understand."

Mom sat up with me in the living room that night. We kept the cat carrier, with Mantha alone inside, next to us. Mom dozed on the couch, but I didn't sleep all night. I watched a DVD of *I Love Lucy* shows. I didn't laugh like I usually do, but I wasn't crying, either. I was too stunned. Could it be true? Did this awful thing really happen?

The next day we had a funeral for Jess. I carried the shoe box with Jess's body to the backyard. I lifted the lid and, for a moment, looked at the small, still body. It looked familiar yet strange somehow. I'd never been around death, and I expected it would look like sleeping. It does, but it's different, too, more like when a candle goes out. Something is missing, the spark.

Dad asked if either of the boys wanted to take a last look. They both shook their heads no.

I had cut a sleeve off the flannel nightgown from the squirrels' first nest. I placed it over Jess and put the lid on the shoe box. We stood around the hole that Dad had dug.

"God bless our little friend," Mom said. We all nodded our heads.

As Dad shoveled dirt into the hole, Charley kept wiping his nose on his sleeve. Jack was the quietest he's ever been in his life.

When the hole was filled, the earth forming a rounded shelter over our Jess, I placed a bouquet of wildflowers on top. We stood quietly for a few more minutes before heading slowly back to the house.

After our short, sweet ceremony, we sat on the porch with Mantha and talked about Jess.

"Remember when Charley said it was raining squirrels after Jess fell out of the tree?" Jack asked.

We smiled and nodded.

"What are your special memories, Nell?" Dad asked.

"I remember how it tickled when he'd sit on my shoulder and stick his nose in my ear. And how he took some of my hair for their nest."

"I remember how Jess liked to climb into my shirt pocket when he was real little," Charley said.

"And I remember how his fur stuck up behind his ears, just like my hair sticks up." Jack patted his cowlick.

"Kids, things happen that we can't explain, let alone understand," Dad said. "But if there's one thing I want you to know for sure, it's that, just because something happens in our lives, it doesn't mean we caused it or that it is our fault. Sometimes bad things just happen. You should all feel good about how you took care of Jess."

"And it's okay to cry," Mom said. "We have a good reason to feel sad. An animal we loved very much is gone. We'll miss Jess."

"Do you think Mantha misses Jess?" Charley asked.

Mantha was sitting on top of the branch in the corner of the porch. She had been there since we came out.

"It's impossible to know what's in Mantha's mind," Dad said. "But I believe Mantha is aware that Jess is gone. In her own way, she probably does miss him."

For the first time since Jess died, I cried.

FOURTEEN

It took me a few days to let Libby know what had happened. When I finally did write, Libby didn't say I'd done anything wrong. She just mourned with me. She told me of a special little squirrel of hers that was killed by a Doberman pinscher shortly after its release. Then she wrote:

> It hurts a lot, Nell. But remember that Jess would have died that first day he fell out of the tree if it hadn't been for you. Instead, he was warm and fed and loved. You made a difference in his life, and he made a difference in yours. That's a lot to say for such a short lifetime. Feel good for what you had and what you did. You did your best for that little guy.

But did I?

FIFTEEN

For days after Jess died, everything felt different and unreal. Places that used to be comfortable—like the screened porch—weren't now. There was a queasy, kind of carsick feeling in my stomach all the time.

I didn't know if I had done the right thing for Jess. And I had to really think about what was best for Mantha.

Mantha was still smaller than an adult squirrel, but not much. I knew it wouldn't be long until she was old enough to live on her own. As much as I hated it, I thought about releasing her. Even though I'd always thought of the indoors as giving protection, maybe it was true that a wild animal was safer outside.

It was up to me to make sure that Mantha was ready to take care of herself. She already had many of the skills she would need to live outside. She had speed to escape danger (like a dog), and she was acrobatic enough to balance on one of my fingers. She could run straight up a brick wall and come down just as fast— headfirst. And she could even stop halfway and, hanging upside down, eat a nut from her front paws.

Her tail had gotten much bushier over the last couple of

weeks. Libby told me that the tail is very important to squirrels because it provides shade and warmth and helps them to balance during those treetop leaps.

A squirrel also uses its tail to communicate. The way a squirrel holds its tail (curled over its body, straight up, or straight back) and the motions it makes with its tail (such as flicking it back and forth) mean different things: curiosity, friendliness, a warning, even anger.

But that isn't the only way squirrels communicate.

One morning I was practicing the piano when I heard a weird sound coming from the porch. I thought maybe Wendell had managed to get in and was attacking Mantha. I stepped on Murphy's tail as I ran to the porch, and I didn't even stop to see if she was okay as she let out a howl and ran under the couch. I had to make sure Mantha was safe. After Jess's death, I worried about Mantha more than ever.

Mom and the boys came running, too. We found Mantha sitting on the branch, shaking her tail and, it seemed to me, screaming. She didn't look hurt, and there was no obvious danger around.

"Could she be choking?" Jack asked.

I handed her a pecan to check. Mantha took the nut, ate it, and then continued making the noise. It reminded me of a duck quack, but drawn out. It sounded almost sad.

"Listen," said Charley.

Somewhere, not too far off, something was making the exact same sound.

"I don't know what it means," Mom said, "but I think Mantha just said her first word."

It was a sound I would hear again many, many times. But it would be awhile before I knew what it meant.

SIXTEEN

About a week after Jess's death, another problem came up. A big one.

The boys and I were doing yard work when Constance Fleagle—owner of Wendell the cat—came charging down the street toward us.

"All of you are in trouble!" she snapped.

I was not in the mood for an argument, especially one with Constance. She's only nine years old, but she's a major know-it-all.

"I don't know what you're talking about. Do you?" Jack challenged her, every bit as smart-alecky as she was. He's always ready to argue, but Constance really sets him off. They've never gotten along. Actually, I can't think of *anyone* who gets along with Constance.

"Oh, I know, all right," she said, standing with her hands on her hips, and her chest and chin pushed out. She flipped her long, perfectly combed blonde hair over the shoulder of her perfectly ironed white blouse. School had just let out for the summer, and no other kid I knew, probably no other kid in the world, would dress like that to play. "My father says what you're doing is illegal!"

"*Please*, don't tell the police that we're weeding the garden again!" Jack pretended to plead.

I started to walk away. I didn't know what Constance was talking about, either, but I was used to her bragging. It usually didn't amount to anything.

"For your information," she announced, "people aren't allowed to keep wild animals. The police could take that 'limb rat' of yours and destroy it!" She sounded like Elmira Gulch coming after Toto in *The Wizard of Oz*.

My jaw dropped to my chest.

"I'm sure you're a genius and an expert on the law and a princess and all that, but you don't know *everything*." Jack tugged hard on the bill of his cap.

"I'm right!" Constance said with a stomp. "You'll see. I might just call the police myself!" She spun on her heel, flipped her hair, and strutted up the sidewalk.

Jack must have been upset because he let her have the last word.

Charley turned to me, a terrified look on his face. "Is that true? Could the police kill Mantha?"

"I don't know, Charley, but I'll find out. Please, don't say anything to anyone, especially not Mom or Dad."

Both boys agreed. They were as afraid as I was.

I wondered how the Fleagles found out about Mantha. Then it came to me: Greta. She had told Joey and Russ about the squirrels. She probably told Constance one day while they were standing at the bus stop. And Constance told her father.

I tried to calm myself so I could think. I remembered Libby's words in her first e-mail: "In many states there are laws against this." But Libby herself had raised squirrels, even when she was only thirteen years old. What difference did it make, anyway? Did the police really care about a squirrel?

I had to figure out what to do. I was afraid to leave Mantha on the porch, but it raised questions when I brought her in the house. Dad was at work, so I went to find Mom. She was in her office, a tiny area next to the living room barely big enough for a desk and chair.

"What's up, Nell?" she asked, looking over.

"I finished weeding the flower bed," I said. "I'm going to my room to read."

"Are your brothers still picking up sticks?"

"They're almost done. Jack said Nathan's coming over to practice batting." Nathan is Joey's brother from the team. Now that it was summer vacation, he'd be over a lot. "And they'll make Charley—I mean, *let* Charley—run after the balls." I tried to make a joke, hoping Mom wouldn't notice how nervous I was.

"Yep, that'll keep them busy," Mom said. "I'm working on a deadline, and I need a few hours of peace. Help me keep an eye on things, okay?"

"Sure," I said. But I was thinking this gave me a little time to do what I had to do. I felt like a criminal as I put Mantha in her carrier and snuck her up to my bedroom. She didn't like to be in the carrier anymore, but I couldn't worry about that now.

I'd never asked Libby what laws she was talking about in that e-mail, and I never tried to find out on my own. I hadn't wanted to learn or do anything that might stop me from keeping the squirrels. I'd lied to Libby and my parents. If Mr. Fleagle knew about Mantha, that could all come out.

It was early afternoon. If Mr. Fleagle decided to talk with Dad, it could happen as soon as 6:00, when Dad came home from work. I needed a plan for how to fix things before then.

For once, I didn't want to go online to search for answers. I needed to talk to a human being. But who could I ask without causing more problems?

If I asked Libby about the law now, after all this time, she'd probably want to know why. She thought I lived out in the country, and that no one else even knew about Mantha. I wondered if I could trick her into thinking I was suddenly just curious. The idea made me ashamed. Somehow, maybe because I never saw her face or heard her voice, it had been so easy for me to lie to Libby. I hadn't given it much thought, even though she had been really nice and had helped me. I didn't want to tell her more lies. But I wasn't ready to tell her the truth, either.

There was someone else I could ask—Russ, who knew a lot about wild animals. Still, I wasn't sure I could trust him. The first time we met he said I should release the squirrels. Would he even want to help me, or would he just say, "I told you so"?

But I couldn't think of another choice, and I had to protect Mantha. Now.

I picked up the phone and looked at it. I'd never called a boy before, let alone Russ. I didn't know what to say.

I called information to get his phone number.

"City and state, please," said a robotic voice.

"Meadowlake, Ohio."

In a few seconds, a human voice said, "May I help you?"

"Do you have a listing for Cason on Sheffield Road?" I asked.

"One moment, please."

Another automated voice came on with a number. I scribbled it down, but it was fifteen minutes before I could talk myself into dialing.

After three rings, a woman answered the phone—Russ's mother, I guessed.

"Um . . . Is Russ there . . . um . . . please?"

There was a pause. Was she waiting for me to tell her who I was? Then she said, "Just a minute." She must have put her hand over the phone because her voice sounded muffled and far away when she called out, "Russ!" A few seconds later, she said in a quiet but excited voice, "It's a girl!"

I wanted to die.

"Hello?"

"Uh, Russ?"

"Yeah."

"Uh . . . hi . . . hi! Uh . . . This is Nell."

"Hi, Nell."

"Um, I have a question. I don't know who to ask, because . . . well, because . . . well, because I don't know who to ask."

"Is something wrong?"

Was it my imagination or did he sound surprised that I'd called? What was I thinking? Of course, he was surprised, *I* was surprised!

"Yeah, I think so. It's private, though. Can anyone hear us?"

"No, go ahead."

I told him about Constance. "It seems like you know a lot about nature and stuff. So, do you know if that's true? Could the police really come here and kill my squirrel?"

"I don't know, but I think I can find out," Russ said. "My grandfather is a retired police officer in Michigan. I'll call and ask him."

"Please don't tell the police who I am!"

"I don't have to tell him your name or anything like that, and he's really nice. It'll be all right."

"Russ?"

"Yeah?"

"Thanks."

"It's okay," he said. "I'll come over to your house after I talk to him."

"Don't knock on the door," I said. "Come to the back porch."

I waited nervously for Russ. I left Mantha in her carrier, just in case I had to grab her and run—where, I didn't know. She hated being locked up. She put her front paws against the metal-grate door and moved quickly from side to side, frantic to get out. I talked to her soothingly and tried to distract her with pecans and Cheerios.

Russ arrived less than a half-hour later. Mom was still working, and Jack, Charley, and Nathan were playing noisily in the yard. Russ and I could talk without being overheard. I opened the door to let him inside and locked it behind him.

"Hi," I said.

"How are you doing? You sounded a little panicky on the phone."

"I guess I am."

"Is anything in here?" He bent to look in Mantha's carrier, which I had faced away from the door in case someone walked up unexpectedly. "Oh, there she is. It *is* a girl, right?"

"Uh-huh."

"What's her name?"

"Samantha, but we call her Mantha."

"Greta told me about the other one. I'm sorry."

I nodded, but it made me more worried to think of Greta blabbing stuff all over town. Maybe I should have told her the truth from the beginning—about wildlife rehabilitators and how I didn't want to find one—so she'd know to keep her mouth shut.

"Can I let her out?" Russ asked.

"Sure."

He sat on the floor and opened the door of the carrier. Mantha immediately climbed to his shoulder. Russ took a couple of walnuts from his shirt pocket and handed one to her. Mantha ate the nut, then leaned down and stuck her nose into his pocket looking for more. Russ laughed and gave her another one. It was nice that he thought to bring something for her. And he had really sounded sorry about Jess. I couldn't figure this guy out.

"Okay, here's what my grandfather told me," he said. "It's against the law in most states, including Ohio, to keep 'native wildlife' without a permit. That means any wild animal that was born here. Mantha *could* be taken away, even put to sleep." He paused to see how I was taking the news. "There could be fines, too. Grampa didn't know if you'd be able to get a permit, especially since you live in a neighborhood—instead of out in the country or someplace like that."

"How could there be such terrible laws?" I was fighting not to cry. "Why would it be against the law to help a baby squirrel dying in your own yard?"

"You can help it. Just not keep it," Russ said quietly. "It's for the animal's own good. And, really, it's best for people, too."

I wasn't sure what he meant, but it was hard to listen to what he was saying. I didn't want to ask more questions. Plus, I was afraid I might start crying.

"Nell, you could release Mantha right now. She's big enough to make it on her own."

I knew this was true. And it was a good thing, because it was probably my only choice to keep Mantha safe.

"I have some chores to do before dinner," he said. "I should go."

"Thanks for coming over . . . and for your help."

Russ smiled at me as he got up to leave. I'd almost forgotten about those blue eyes.

"See ya," he said.

"See ya."

I turned toward Mantha, sitting on the branch grooming her tail. I loved her, and I knew what I had to do. As much as I hated the idea, releasing her was the right thing. And it had to happen soon.

Should I do it right then? Just open the door . . .

But I couldn't. Not yet. *I* wasn't ready.

I'd do it tomorrow. Or no later than the day after that. . . .

Mr. Fleagle didn't stop by that night, but I knew that, at any time, he could—just as Constance had—and tell Mom and Dad about how I was breaking the law.

Or maybe the police would just show up to take Mantha away.

SEVENTEEN

The first thing I wanted to do before I released Mantha was let her practice more climbing. Libby had told me awhile back to take the squirrels out and let them play on the trees. Instead, I had moved them to the screened porch. Climbing hadn't seemed so important then, when I still secretly hoped the squirrels would live with me forever.

The next morning, after breakfast and schoolwork, Jack and Charley came with me as I took Mantha in her carrier out to the ash tree—the same tree she had fallen out of about ten weeks before. This was just a warm-up, so it would be good to have extra hands around in case she tried to get away.

Jack and Charley stood on either side of me as I put Mantha at the bottom of the trunk. But even with all of us standing right there, she quickly climbed out of reach.

"Man! She's fast!" Jack jumped up, trying to catch her. Charley rushed off to get Mom.

I wondered if this was the last time I'd ever see Mantha. I knew the moment was coming, fast, but I ached at the thought that this was the end.

Charley and Mom ran over to the tree.

"What's going on?" Mom asked. She must have been very surprised by the sight of the empty carrier in the yard and Mantha at the top of the tree. I hadn't wanted to tell Mom first, even though she would have understood, in case she asked questions. I didn't want to talk about it. I thought we'd just give Mantha a few minutes on the tree and be back on the porch before Mom ever knew what was happening.

"Libby told me I should let Mantha get used to climbing on trees," I explained, "so she'd be ready for release soon."

"That's wonderful!" Mom said.

"But I didn't think she'd get away from us so fast."

"We were only letting her practice," Charley said. "We didn't mean to let her go!"

"She'll come down," Mom said, walking back to the house. "She's enjoying herself! And she's not in any danger."

Mantha *was* having fun. She ran back and forth on nearly every limb of the ash tree. She finally did run down, but immediately raced across the yard and up the oak tree.

She was still making a grand tour of the yard when she caught the attention of another squirrel. He—I guessed it was a male because he seemed so big next to Mantha—made a dash after her.

"Hey, leave her alone," Jack yelled. "Go away!"

But the big squirrel wasn't bothered by us. He chased Mantha up and down and around and around the trunk of the ash tree. Mantha was doing a pretty good job of keeping away from him, until she ran out on a limb. She went out to the very tip with the other squirrel right behind her. The branch bent low under their weight. Mantha lost her balance and tumbled to the ground—a very big drop!

We ran over to see if she was okay, and she let me pick her up. I took her to the screened porch, so glad to have her in my arms again. Back on the porch, Mantha seemed like her old self. She wasn't hurt, and she gobbled up all of our pecans. Then she curled up on my lap for a nap.

"I don't think she's quite ready to live outside yet," I told the boys. "Maybe we'll release her in a few more days."

But Mantha soon let us know otherwise. Almost the second she woke up, she wanted to go back out. She jumped onto the screen door and ran up and down. She acted like . . . well, like a wild animal. One that was suddenly trapped.

I opened the door.

EIGHTEEN

That afternoon, Mantha began building a nest in the oak tree in our side yard. She picked a spot in the lowest part of the tree, so she had to climb higher to get materials to work with. She bit off twigs with bunches of leaves attached and carried them down a large main branch. She was holding her head high as she made her way back, but she kept stepping on the leaves, causing her to slip and slide down long sections of the steep limb.

"It's like squirrel skateboarding." Jack laughed.

"Or tree surfing," I said.

Mantha was building in a wide fork of the tree, which unfortunately didn't help much in holding the nest together. She would try to anchor one clump of leaves to the heap, but no sooner did she turn to go after more when a large section of her work would tumble down. Twice as many leaves ended up on the ground as in the nest.

"Too bad Jess isn't here to help her," I said sadly.

"Should we try to stop her?" Charley asked.

"I wouldn't know how," I said. "And we shouldn't."

"Are we really letting her go, then?"

"I guess so," I admitted. "Constance was right. I think we have to release Mantha."

"Do Mom and Dad know—about the law, I mean?" Jack asked.

"No, and I think that's best—at least for now. Okay?" Jack didn't even try to argue. The boys knew how upset our parents would be by the news. None of us wanted to see that.

"Your friends are coming." Charley pointed down the street.

Greta was walking up the sidewalk with Joey and Russ. Lately, it seemed that I never saw Greta without Joey, and Russ was with them more and more. I wondered if he had told them about our conversation the day before. I had forgotten to ask him to keep it a secret.

"Hey! We're going to a movie to celebrate summer vacation," Greta said. "Want to come with us?"

"Thanks, but I have my own show going on here." I nodded toward the tree.

"Is that *Mantha?*" Greta was shocked. "I didn't know you were letting her go so soon!"

"I didn't, either," I said, glancing at Russ.

"You guys never got to meet Mantha before, did you?" Greta asked Russ and Joey.

That answered my question about whether Russ had told them.

"Nope! And now she's all grown-up and moving out on her own. Big day, isn't it, Mom?" Joey teased me.

I wasn't ready to laugh about it yet.

"You okay, Nell?" Russ asked.

"I guess so."

"How about Mantha?"

"Well, she was chased by a giant squirrel and fell out of a tree."

"Great start!" said Joey.

"She looks pretty good, though," said Russ. "She knows what to do."

"Yeah, I guess," I said. "She came in to eat and took a nap, but then she wanted to go back out. It was like I couldn't keep her inside anymore. And now she's been building this nest for a while."

"You mean that pile of leaves is a nest?" Joey asked.

"The one in the tree, not the one on the ground!" I told him.

They laughed. Greta pulled her camera from her pocket and started snapping pictures, circling the trunk of the tree to get different angles. She even lay on her back under the spot where Mantha was building.

"It's lucky she didn't move far away from you," Greta said between shots.

"Not yet, anyway."

"Did you know she could do this? This nest-building thing?"

"No. It's kind of amazing, isn't it?"

Mantha's instincts told her to build a nest on her first day outside. How did she know it had to be in the trees or what to make it from? Did she remember the nest she had fallen out of as a baby?

In another minute or two, Mantha decided the nest was finished and crawled inside. It was late afternoon, much earlier than she usually went to sleep.

"I hope she doesn't want to stay in there all night." I wondered if the nest would stay in one piece that long. To make things worse, the sky looked like it was going to rain.

"Why else did you think she was building it?" Russ asked.

I shrugged.

"We have to get going," Joey said.

"Come with us, Nell," Greta urged.

"No, you guys go on."

"There's nothing you can do," Russ said.

"Probably not, but I want to be here."

Mom stepped onto the front porch to get the mail. "This looks like an important gathering," she joked. "Are you collecting money or signatures?"

"We're trying to get Nell to go to a movie with us," Greta told her.

"I'll donate to that cause!" Mom said.

Everyone looked at me, but I shook my head. "Not today."

"We'd better leave, then. I guess I'll see you tomorrow." Greta waved good-bye.

I nodded and waved as the three of them walked down the street.

"Nell," Mom said, "go with them!"

I shook my head again.

"You should be spending time with your friends, not moping around after a squirrel!"

"I will. Soon. Summer's just starting."

Mom sighed and went in the house.

It began to drizzle. I put a pile of pecans and sunflower seeds in Mantha's carrier, hoping I could coax her down and onto the screened porch. I stood under the tree, calling her name. But I couldn't even get her to look at me. She was probably already asleep after her big day.

"Nell, come in out of the rain," Mom called. "Please!"

"I don't think her nest is very sturdy."

"If it isn't, she'll know what to do."

Dad pulled into the driveway, and I decided to go inside. If Mom was a little annoyed with me, Dad would be a lot more. At least it wasn't raining too hard.

Dad was thrilled when he heard about Mantha. "This is the best news! I thought we'd have to force you to release her."

"I told you I had a plan."

"I shouldn't have doubted it." He beamed. "I'm so proud of your mature, responsible attitude."

I felt terrible listening to praise I didn't deserve, so I went to my room.

I considered sending an e-mail to Libby, telling her that Mantha was officially living outside, but I was afraid she'd be curious about why I had released her earlier than we had discussed. I decided not to write for a while, unless Libby wrote to me first. I hoped nothing bad happened in the meantime that I might need her help with.

After dinner, the rain turned into a heavy downpour, and I grew more nervous. I put on my raincoat and went outside. Again, I stood under the tree calling Mantha. With the rain hitting my plastic hood, I couldn't hear if she was moving, and I could barely keep my eyes open as I turned my face upward.

I returned to the house, and Dad said, "Good, I'm glad you came in. I know this is new and you're a little worried, but Mantha will be fine. You don't want to stand out there in that mess."

"I just came in for these," I told him, putting on my sunglasses. He looked puzzled but didn't try to stop me from going back out. My parents were trying to be understanding, but even my brothers thought I was acting weird.

"You look psycho," Jack said.

The sunglasses helped me keep my eyes open in the rain. But it was too dark to see anything, and I could have used some windshield wipers. Plus, rain was running down my neck into my shirt. My clothes and shoes were sopping wet. I was miserable.

I had to admit it was hopeless. I left the porch door open a crack—just in case Mantha changed her mind. I went to bed with the feeling that I'd never see her again, at least not in the same way—up close, on my lap, wanting to be with me. What if she always avoided me now, afraid that I'd lock her inside again? Or what if she left the yard or even the neighborhood? How would I ever know where she was?

I got up at 6 a.m. when I heard Mom go downstairs. It was still raining. We looked out the window. "I don't see her," Mom said, opening the door.

I headed back to my room. I wanted to be alone to cry. Then I heard, "Well, look who's here!"

I turned to see a soaking-wet squirrel sitting on Mom's shoulder.

NINETEEN

I think Mantha had been happy living in the house. But once she knew the difference, it was clear she wanted to be outside. She made visits to the porch several times each day to get something to eat, even though she seemed to be finding food outside on her own, too. Then she'd go straight to the door to be let out. And you did not want to keep her waiting. Whenever she felt caged, she made sharp, hard moves—leaping on or off of me with powerful lunges or running quickly down my back and legs. The squirrel tracks she left were painful, and they upset my mother more than ever. Now that Mantha was living outside, Mom was really worried about infected scratches. I learned it was better if I went out into the yard to see Mantha. That way, I could have a longer, calmer visit.

In some ways, things hadn't changed much. I still saw Mantha many times every day. But we weren't breaking the law anymore.

One day, while I was taking trash to the cans behind the garage, Mantha ran up to me and crawled onto my shoulder. I sat on the ground, and she stretched out on my lap to sleep. As I stroked her side, like I used to do when she and Jess were babies,

I became aware of some sort of animal call. I had been more tuned in to nature sounds since I began keeping my life list. I looked around for the bird or animal making the cry.

Then I saw something more urgent: Wendell was in Mrs. Brumley's yard!

"Mantha, wake up. There's a cat coming." I carried her to the ash tree and put her on the trunk.

Wendell calmly walked up and rubbed against my legs. I ignored his attempts to get my attention—I couldn't forgive his hunting and killing, even if it wasn't his fault—and I sat under the tree to wait until he left. I heard a noise above me. I looked up and saw that Mantha had crawled out onto a limb right over Wendell and was crying out. It sounded like *qua-a-a-a-a*.

That was the same odd sound we'd heard Mantha making the day I thought she was being attacked on the porch. Mom had called it Mantha's "first word." And it was the same animal call I'd just heard, right before I noticed Wendell. Did it mean what I thought? Was it some kind of alarm for other squirrels—a warning that there was a cat in the area?

I couldn't wait for it to happen again to see if I was right. So the next day, I decided to test my theory.

Our cat Murphy always tries to get out during warm months. We don't want her to hunt like Wendell does, so we keep her indoors. But we can't stop her from trying to go outside. She crouches next to the door, ready to escape if we give her the chance. We never do, so she must have been surprised when I picked her up and carried her out to the yard.

I put her down and sat in the grass to listen.

It wasn't long before I heard the cry. I saw a squirrel on Mrs. Brumley's garage roof, near where Murphy was rolling in the grass. It looked straight at Murphy and called, *Qua-a-a-a-a!* The squirrel held its tail—which was all fluffed out—high in the air and flicked it front to back and side to side. When Murphy got up and walked across the yard, the squirrel got even more excited: *Kuk-kuk-kuk*, it scolded as it shook its tail.

I brought Murphy back in the house, and the noise stopped.

I was right.

Although Mantha warned other squirrels when she saw a cat, she still wasn't friendly to the squirrels and chased them from our yard. Squirrels aren't social animals. But other squirrels figured out when we were giving Mantha treats. They'd creep up to see if they could get food, too, and I was happy to give them some. Mantha eventually got used to sharing.

Once while the boys and I were feeding the squirrels, a blue jay landed on our basketball hoop over the garage door and cocked his head to the side, watching the action.

"Do you think the blue jay wants a peanut?" Charley asked.

"I'll throw him one." Jack tossed a peanut high in the air, and the bird swooped down and caught it before it hit the ground. The blue jay cracked the shell against the basketball hoop and gobbled up the nut.

"Awesome! What a great trick," Charley said.

We threw another peanut and another and another.

"He's a good catcher," Jack said.

"Better than anybody playing for the Bearcats," I teased.

"Ha-ha. You're so funny."

After that, whenever we'd call Mantha to visit and, of course, eat, there was the blue jay on the basketball hoop, cocking his head and waiting his turn.

Another bird got our attention during Mantha's first weeks outside: a very angry robin, which would sit on a limb, watching, as Mantha dug around in the yard. Then it would dive directly at her, within inches of her head.

I finally wrote and told Libby about Mantha moving out. She responded soon.

> I'm so proud, Nell! I know it must have been difficult, but you're doing all the right things. Keep it up!

She wouldn't have said that if she knew the whole story of why I released Mantha and that I'd been keeping it a secret from her for two weeks. But I hoped that I *was* on the right track now and that the lies were behind me at last.

I asked Libby what Mantha could have done to make a robin so mad at her. She wrote:

> Squirrels sometimes raid birds' nests and eat the eggs or hatchlings (baby birds). But usually they eat meat only if there's no other food. Mantha has plenty to eat, so I hope she isn't eating baby birds!

Whatever the reason, the robin kept up the attacks for three days. Mantha acted like it didn't bother her—she never tried to run away—but she did seem to spend more time under bushes and tall plants.

Mantha had many ways of getting out of trouble. She could leap from a branch to the rooftop and back again. She could run along telephone or electric wires. I thought this was an amazing feat, until one day, during a power outage, I overheard an electric company worker tell Dad it was probably caused by a squirrel "getting fried on some transformer."

But the biggest danger for Mantha was the street in front of our house. We don't live on a really busy street; there's just the usual neighborhood traffic. But that's bad enough, because none of Mantha's skills could protect her from cars. And I couldn't protect her, either. The only thing I could do if I saw her in the road was to go inside. If I did anything that distracted her, she might stop in the street, and even a moment might be too long.

TWENTY

Because I spent a lot of time with a squirrel, I noticed that not everyone thinks they're as cute and wonderful as I do. Some people hate squirrels.

Our neighbor Mrs. Brumley throws stones at them. Whenever she saw me with Mantha, she'd glare at me like I was spreading the plague. Sometimes she'd call out things like "Does your mother know you let that filthy animal jump on you?" Or she might simply shake her head and say, "miserable limb rat," which I've learned is the Number One insult against squirrels.

I couldn't understand it.

Libby explained:

> Squirrels dig in vegetable and flower gardens. They chew on tree limbs and bark. In the winter, a squirrel may decide to move into your attic or basement and will chew up and shred things, including wiring, on the way in.

And that was from a person who loves squirrels!

Dad must have expected that once we released her, Mantha would move out into the world and we'd never see her again. Our lives would return to "normal." As far as Dad was concerned, Mantha had pretty much worn out her welcome.

"Squirrels are troublemakers," Dad said. "Lots of people try to get rid of them, or discourage them from coming into their yards. Look at all the problems Mantha causes me! She empties the birdfeeders as fast as I can fill them, digs up my tulip bulbs, and leaves dozens of little holes in the yard where she buries things. Frankly, I don't blame Mrs. Brumley for being upset when she sees you feeding squirrels and encouraging them to come here."

Who knew things could get worse?

One morning, Mom took Jack to the dentist to get his chipped tooth fixed. I was on the back porch watching Charley, who was on the tire swing eating a grape Popsicle. Mantha showed up and began chasing Charley's feet. I came out for a closer look, because it was really funny. Charley kept changing directions and spinning around in circles, and Mantha followed right along. Suddenly, Charley came to a stop. Mantha ran up his leg and sat on the top of the swing, so they were eye to eye. Then she reached out with her front paws and took the Popsicle away from him! She took a small bite, then gobbled up the final inch of dripping purple ice.

We were laughing so hard that I almost didn't hear, "Can I play?" It was Adrian Sanchez, the five-year-old who lives in the house behind us. He's a sweet kid with soft brown curls and huge brown eyes.

I saw Mrs. Sanchez standing on their porch. I waved to let her know it was fine for Adrian to stay; she waved back.

"Do you want to ride on the swing?" I asked him. "Just give me a minute." I handed a pecan to Mantha so I could get the gooey Popsicle stick away from her.

"Is that *your* squirrel?" Adrian asked.

"Kind of," I said.

"I want to feed it!"

"No, Adrian."

"I won't hurt it."

"I know you won't, but only big kids are allowed to feed it. You're too little."

"I want to," he whined. "Pleeeease?"

"Sorry!"

"Pleeeease?" he asked, louder. "You did it. Why can't I? PLEEEEEEEASE?"

I took a pecan from my pocket. It really didn't seem like that big of a deal, not while I was standing right there watching. "Well," I said, handing him the nut, "can you be careful? Hold your hand just like this and don't move." I showed him to lay the pecan in his palm.

He held his hand up to Mantha, who was still sitting on the top of the tire swing. But when she tried to take the pecan, Adrian got scared and pulled it away from her.

"Here, let me do it."

"I can do it!" he said. He reached out again, but this time he was pinching the nut between his index finger and thumb. Before I could say or do anything, Mantha lunged for the nut with her mouth. Adrian squealed loudly, and Mantha ran up the tree trunk—with the pecan in her jaws. Luckily, there was no break in Adrian's skin, no sign of blood, not even a scratch. Mantha mostly just scared him, I thought. But that didn't stop Adrian from screaming and screaming like his whole finger had been bitten off.

"Adrian, what's wrong?" Mrs. Sanchez called as she ran across the yard.

"That squirrel bit me!" Adrian howled, pointing at Mantha. "I was giving it a nut, and it bit me!"

His mother raced toward us as fast as I've ever seen a human move. There was a look of terror on her face.

"I'm sorry!" I said. "He isn't really hurt. He begged me to feed her!"

"Let me see," she said soothingly, looking at Adrian's finger. "Aw, sweetie, you're fine. Come inside. We'll clean you up."

Then she looked at me, furious. "Wait right here! I want to talk to you."

Charley and I waited in silence. I hoped Mom wouldn't get home before Mrs. Sanchez returned. As bad as things were now . . .

Fortunately, Mantha was gone when Adrian and his mother came back out. Adrian had a cookie in his hand and a Band-Aid on his finger, which he was holding straight up, like it was in a cast or something.

Little twerp, I thought.

"What happened?" Mrs. Sanchez demanded.

I didn't want to tell her too much about how I'd raised Mantha. On the other hand, wouldn't that be better than her thinking I'd let her son feed a totally wild animal? I tried to stay in the middle.

"We know that squirrel," I said. "We feed her all the time, and she's very, very gentle. Adrian saw me feed her, and he *begged* me to do it, too. She didn't mean to nip at him, but he jerked the nut away from her. . . . It was all my fault, and I am so, so sorry."

"You should be! You absolutely should have known better," she stressed. "Adrian can be strong-willed, but that is no excuse for what you did. How could you let a wild animal get that close to a little child? Not to mention *feeding* it? How incredibly dangerous!"

"I'm sorry," I said again.

"I'm sure you are, but— Where are your parents?"

Gulp.

"Dad's at work, and Mom took Jack to the dentist."

"I don't even know what to do." She was close to tears. "First, I realize that Adrian is not hurt, so we are very, very lucky. But a bite would have been extremely serious. Do you know about rabies?"

"Yes," I said, trying to calm her down. "But squirrels almost NEVER get rabies. I can show you online—"

"*Almost!* Let me tell you what *I* know about rabies. A wild animal with rabies doesn't act like a healthy animal. It acts friendly and unafraid. So a squirrel that comes up to people is already suspicious. Someone might call the police or wildlife officials if they saw your squirrel acting that way. And if there were a bite! A bite would *have* to be reported, and your squirrel would be taken away—rabies or not. Do you understand what I'm telling you?"

"Yes, I do."

Charley's eyes were frightened. I wished he would go inside, where he couldn't hear her.

Mrs. Sanchez sighed. "I'm sorry, Nell. I don't want to scare you. I just don't know . . ."

She looked almost as sad as she was angry. She turned and went home.

I knew I couldn't brush this incident away without saying something to Mom. When the car pulled into the driveway, I told Charley, "Leave *all* of the talking to me."

Jack's tooth was still chipped, so I asked about that first.

"They took a mold," Mom explained. "He'll have a porcelain veneer ready in a couple of weeks to cover the tooth, and his smile will be as good as new. What's been going on here?"

"Well . . ." I took a deep breath, which was a mistake. I had intended to make the story sound like it was just a little thing, but now Mom was looking at me like I was about to deliver bad news.

"What, Nell? Is something wrong?"

"No, no, not really," I said, "but Adrian was over, and Mantha was here, too."

"Oh, no!"

"It's nothing! He was just here, and I was feeding Mantha and—"

"Oh, no!" Mom said louder. "She didn't jump on him and scratch him. Did she?"

"No, he's fine. But she scared him." I skipped over the part about letting Adrian feed her. "I already talked to Mrs. Sanchez." That kind of made it sound like I took responsibility and went over to see her first. "I told her about Mantha, and I think she is pretty cool with it now." I knew *that* was a huge exaggeration.

"You're coming with me right now, and we're going over to talk to Elena!"

I had no choice. I was shaking as we walked through the yard.

When we got to their driveway, Mrs. Sanchez was putting Adrian in his car seat.

"Elena! Hello!" Mom called. "Nell was just telling me what happened. I am so sorry! Is Adrian okay?"

"Yes, yes, he's fine," Mrs. Sanchez said. She actually gave me a small smile. Maybe she was relieved that I'd told my mother and she wouldn't have to. "He has forgotten all about it. We're on our way to the park to meet friends."

"I won't keep you," Mom said. "I just wanted to be sure that you understood about the squirrel, and I promise you that nothing like that will ever happen again. I'll see to it."

"I certainly hope so," Mrs. Sanchez said, but she nodded and smiled again, this time a little bigger. She seemed satisfied for now. "Thank you for coming over. I know you'll do the right thing."

That was it! I think both Mom and Mrs. Sanchez assumed that I had confessed everything there was to know.

After dinner, Dad called us together.

"I heard about what happened this afternoon," he began, "and it made me realize that we haven't taken the time to think about the circumstances of Mantha being outside. We got a taste today of what could occur. We might not be so fortunate the next time.

"So these are the new rules: If anyone else is here, you are not to call or feed Mantha. If she comes around when you are with someone, you come into the house immediately. But we—especially you, Nell—have to pull back. It's important for her to learn not to be dependent on us."

We had escaped complete disaster, but I felt miserable and guilty about putting Mantha in such a bad situation. The threat that neighbors might call my parents—or the police!—had grown.

And now there was yet another reason that I could be in deep, deep trouble if my parents learned the whole truth.

TWENTY-ONE

I was haunted with worries about Mantha. Despite Dad's warning about spending less time with her, more than ever, I needed to be sure she was okay. I didn't have long visits, but each morning, before I started my chores and schoolwork, even before I ate breakfast, I fed Mantha. She knew the routine as well as I did. A minute after I opened the door, sometimes just a few seconds, I'd see her running toward me.

One Saturday morning at the end of June, Mantha didn't come when I went to the door. I wasn't too surprised, because for some reason, I woke up really early that day. Everyone else in the family was still asleep. Usually, I'm the last one up. Then things got even weirder. I didn't see Mantha, but I noticed right away that there were more squirrels than usual in our yard. I counted six on one tree, and four were hanging from the porch screens! There was definitely something strange going on, and it scared me. I thought about an old horror movie Greta and I once watched called *The Birds*, about a small town where the birds flocked together and attacked people. Maybe I was in the middle of *The Squirrels*.

Finally, I spotted Mantha in the side yard. But instead of

111

coming to me, she took off in the other direction. She ran up a tree with maybe ten squirrels right behind her. I couldn't figure out what was going on, but now I was scared for Mantha.

I didn't want to wake my parents. If Mantha was in trouble—again—they might get mad—*again*. Still, I needed help, so I woke up Jack.

When we got outside, Mantha was leading the squirrels in a full-out chase around our yard. She'd bolt up a tree trunk and out to the tip of a branch, then leap to another tree or to the roof of our house or the garage, then onto the next tree. The other squirrels followed her every move.

I thought she might fall and get hurt. Or worse, that the other squirrels might catch her. I couldn't imagine what they'd do to her.

"Man!" Jack hollered. "What's going on?"

"Maybe she did something to get them mad."

"Do you think they want to hurt her?"

I didn't want to say it, but that was exactly what I thought. I ran inside to the linen closet and brought out an old sheet.

"Jack! Grab the other side!" I yelled as I tried to get beneath Mantha.

We criss-crossed the yard, stretching the sheet between us like a fireman's net, in case Mantha fell or wanted to jump to safety. We ran around and around the house, trying to keep up with the squirrels, until, on one trip through the front yard, Jack stopped. He dropped his side of the sheet and flopped to the ground.

"Don't you feel stupid?" he asked. "We must look like idiots."

I was still in my nightgown, my hair in a wild tangle; Jack was wearing too-small pajamas with Spider-Man on his chest; and we were running through the yard in our bare feet with a sheet, trying to catch a squirrel. *Idiot* sounded about right.

But by then I was too worried about Mantha to care what the neighbors thought. I couldn't stop.

"Please, Jack, look how many there are! We have to help her."

"You think this is helping her?"

"You have a better idea?"

Jack slowly stood and picked up the sheet. We began racing again, back and forth, around and around, trying to stay with the pack.

Then, as Jack and I were running in circles in our front yard, the sheet pulled tight between us, we heard loud laughter.

"What are you doing?!" Russ asked. He could barely get the words out. He and Joey got off of their bikes. They rolled on the ground, howling.

What were they doing up and out so early? Then I noticed their fishing poles.

"I can't stand it!" Russ held his stomach.

"She's making me do it!" Jack dropped the sheet again.

"Shut up, Jack. You don't have to explain to them," I said.

"I'm blowing snot bubbles!" Joey snorted. "You're killing me!"

Jack joined Russ and Joey, all of them laughing so hard they couldn't talk anymore.

I sat under a tree. I didn't know what to do next—go back to trying to help Mantha or crawl into a hole.

"You looked like a couple of circus clowns!" Joey finally said. "You know, running around with a trampoline, trying to get the other clown to jump from the burning building. All you needed was a bucket of confetti to throw on us!"

"I'm glad you think this is so funny. Didn't you notice that there is a mob of squirrels chasing Mantha?" I said.

"What do you think they're doing?" Russ asked, wiping tears from his eyes with the palms of his hands.

"Well . . . I don't know exactly. Maybe they're jealous of her."

"Squirrels don't get jealous," he said.

"Look at them! What do *you* think they're doing?" I asked.

"I'd guess they're trying to mate with her," Russ said. "That's what it usually means when a bunch of male animals chase a female."

"She's too young, smarty," I told him.

Mantha was only about four months old. Libby had told me that female squirrels usually mate and have their first babies at about one year old.

"Trust me, Nell. Mantha isn't even a little bit scared of those squirrels."

He did seem to be right about that. Now that I really thought about it, she looked like she was playing. I wanted to run to my room and get on my computer to see if I could learn what was going on. If I hadn't been so worried, I might have thought of that sooner.

"We have to go." Joey got on his bike. "Russ is taking me to his favorite fishing spot. But thanks for the entertainment!"

"We'll check back later!" Russ called to me as they pedaled down the street.

"Don't bother," I mumbled.

After a short online search, I decided Russ was probably right. Mantha was in a "mating dance" with a group of males. She was young, but it was possible, especially since she lived on such a high-quality diet—all the pecans, walnuts, fruits, and vegetables I gave her. Her good health made her very mature for her age.

A few hours later, there were only four squirrels chasing Mantha. By the end of the afternoon, it was down to two.

When I went in the house at dinnertime, just one guy was

left, and he looked tired. He and Mantha were sitting quietly in the ash tree. Mantha was grooming herself on a very narrow limb, ignoring him. The male couldn't get any closer to her without the limb bending under their weight. If he tried to reach her, they'd probably fall. So he just lay on the branch facing Mantha, softly crying out.

When I came back out after dinner, they were both gone.

TWENTY-TWO

Greta had collected hundreds of pictures of Mantha. Dad gave her special privileges to be around Mantha, both because he wanted to encourage her photography and because Greta had been around since Mantha was little. With school out, Greta came over with her camera more often. And wherever Greta was, Joey would soon show up, too, usually with Russ.

"Just watch the close-ups when the guys are here," Dad told us. "Don't call Mantha over."

"I'll use the zoom," Greta promised.

We spent a lot of time watching Greta take pictures of Mantha. It didn't bother me, but the guys started to get bored.

"Why don't you take pictures of something else?" Joey groaned one day. "Anything else. Why is it always Mantha?"

"I want to be a wildlife photographer," Greta said, "and she's wildlife."

"How about other animals—like wildlife that is actually wild?" Russ suggested. "You should try shooting more of a moving target."

"Those might not be the best words to use—I mean,

coming from a hunter," I said, but I was teasing.

"You two still arguing about that stuff?" Joey laughed.

"Of course!"

"Let me try that again," Russ said, grinning. "Why don't you take pictures of animals that act less tame? Is that better, Nell?"

"Better."

"I don't normally run into other wild animals in Meadowlake," Greta said. "I have some pretty good shots of birds, but that's about it."

"How about we go to Glenecho?" Joey asked excitedly. "There would be animals there. Right, Russ?"

"Absolutely!"

Glenecho Nature Preserve is just outside Meadowlake. Mom takes us there a lot, and ten of the birds on my life list were spotted there.

I went to ask my mom while the others called theirs. I found her in the dining room working on math with the boys.

"Sure!" she said. "That's a terrific idea." She and Dad had not made it a secret that they wanted me to spend less time with squirrels and more time with people.

We began the nearly mile-long walk to Glenecho. It was a hot day, and we were all soaked with sweat as we arrived at the entrance. But as soon as we stepped into the shadows of the trees, it was much cooler.

"Nature's air conditioning!" Russ said. "That feels good."

Russ pointed out things along the trail for Greta to photograph: wildflowers (which he knew by name), spiderwebs in the bushes, and tadpoles and minnows in the creek.

"This is all great," Greta said. "But you promised me wild animals. Scare some up for me!"

"They're here," Russ said. "We just have to be quiet—and wait."

"Do you know what kinds of animals live here?" asked Joey.

"Well, I've heard there are more than a hundred species of birds, including several kinds of owls, which are my favorites," Russ said.

I felt humbled about the mere ten I had added to my list.

"There are at least a couple kinds of squirrels—for Nell." He nodded at me. "Plus, chipmunks, rabbits, groundhogs, raccoons, voles, and bats. I'm sure there are frogs and turtles and snakes. Probably hundreds of deer. Maybe some foxes. Millions of bugs. And lots of other things that I'm forgetting right now." He pointed to nests in the trees, bits of fur and feathers here and there on the ground, and even small holes in the bark as proof that plenty of animals lived nearby.

"Cool!" he said, stooping to pick up something from beneath a fir tree.

"What is it?" I asked.

"An owl pellet." He opened his hand to show us. It was a grayish-brown lump, about the size and shape of a chicken nugget, but furry.

"What's an owl pellet?" Greta asked.

"Owls can't chew, so they swallow their prey whole," Russ explained. "The parts they can't digest—like fur, bones, teeth, and feathers—are compressed into this nice little package. Owls cough up a few of these every day."

"Does that mean you're holding bird puke in your hand?" Joey said.

"Basically." Russ smiled, then he added, "The pellets from

each kind of owl look different. I think this one is from a screech owl."

"Open it up," Joey said. "I want to see if there are any bones in it."

Russ unraveled the pellet. "Here's a jaw bone, probably from a mouse."

I could see tiny teeth. There were at least a dozen other small bones and some fur.

"Where's the owl?" Greta looked up. "Do you see it?"

Russ studied the area. "No, but it's hard to spot an owl."

We moved toward a creek a little way down the path.

"I hope you won't be too disappointed if we don't see many animals," Russ said to Greta, who was leading the way.

"Nah," she said. She turned and smiled but kept walking. I was suddenly struck by how pretty Greta is. She has a great smile and her hair just gleams. Mine is a jumble of frizz. I somehow hadn't noticed before how grown-up Greta looks. She's rounder than I am, softer looking, I mean. I'm bony. I instantly felt like a beanpole, all gangly and awkward. I slumped along behind the others.

"Come on, Nell!" Russ said. "You're not getting tired, are you?"

"No, I'm fine."

He smiled at me. It made me feel a little better.

We did see quite a few squirrels and some birds, and one chipmunk ran across the path in front of us. It's easy to do bird-watching with Russ around. He recognizes them so I didn't have to look them up. I added four new ones to my life list. Greta got some good photos.

As we started for home, we all agreed to come back soon.

Joey and Russ turned off a few blocks earlier than we did, and Greta immediately started to tease me about Russ.

"As much as you two disagree about hunting and all that stuff, you get along great."

"He's okay," I said. "Even if he's completely wrongheaded about some things."

"Uh-huh. He's just 'okay.' You two are so much alike, and you don't even see it!"

As we walked into my yard, Jack and Charley came to the door, yelling, "Hurry! You won't believe it!"

Greta and I rushed inside.

In the kitchen, I spotted something strange on the refrigerator. A Dave! The moths had come out of their cocoons. There were two more between the kitchen and the living room. We found a Dave that was still wet, having just emerged from the cocoon, and its wings hadn't "inflated" yet. Another was just pushing its way through the top of a cocoon in the living room.

"Charley saw the first one come out a couple of hours ago," Mom said. "So we called Ann to come over and tell us more about them."

"What do you kids think?" Ann asked. "Pretty cool, huh?"

Ann is a big person, and I don't mean just in size, although she is tall. She has a big laugh that you hear coming before you see her. She gets really excited about things, and her voice gets bigger and bigger when she talks about stuff she likes.

"They're beautiful!" I said.

"Awesome!" said Charley.

"I can't believe how huge they are," Greta said. "I didn't know moths could be bigger than butterflies."

"These are promethea, and they're not the biggest," Ann told her. "You should see luna moths! They're twice as big."

The Daves were about three or four inches across their wingspans—lots bigger than the moths that hang out by porch lights.

"Can you tell the boys from the girls?" Jack asked. "Maybe they could be the Daves and Davinas now."

Ann laughed. "Yeah, there's a difference. The females have lighter, brighter colors. They're reddish to brown. Like this one. And here's a male. They're dark brown to black. Both males and females have the same tan borders. Do you see these spots in the corners of their wings? They're called *eyespots*. Don't they look a little like eyeballs?"

Dad came in. "Is this a party?"

"Yeah!" cheered Charley. "Do you notice anything?"

"The Daves are out! Then we should definitely celebrate," Dad said.

Mom and Dad fixed root beer floats and popcorn.

Greta was happily snapping pictures. "I still get the best nature shots at your house," she told me. "It's like science class, only a lot better."

I had an idea. I went to one of the Daves and slowly, gently slipped my finger under it. "Everybody get one!"

"What are you doing, Nell?" Mom asked.

"Releasing them!"

"I like the way you think!" said Ann. "Promethea don't have very long life-spans, and they really should enjoy the little time they have in the great outdoors."

There were just enough moths for everybody to have one. We formed a line—a moth parade—out to the yard. We held our hands up in the air and, one by one, the Daves flew away. We watched quietly until they were all out of sight.

TWENTY-THREE

I had noticed a change in Mantha. She was much less friendly, even toward me. She might sit on my shoulder, but not on my lap, and when I'd try to pet her, she'd bat my hand away. A couple of times she nipped at me.

"It's possible that her wild side is coming through more," Mom suggested. "I think she means business! All of you kids need to give her space—especially you, Nell."

I didn't want to, but I thought maybe Mom was right.

One Tuesday morning, when we returned home from my piano lesson, Mantha came running to meet us. She scrambled up to my shoulder, looking for food. Without thinking, Mom reached out to stroke her. Mantha sat up on her back legs, wrapped her front paws around Mom's wrist, and bit down on Mom's index finger. Mantha didn't let go! She still had her back feet on my shoulder, facing away from me, so I grabbed her tail, yanking hard. Mom was able to shake herself free. Mantha dove to the ground and made a beeline for the nearest tree.

In the kitchen, tears streamed down Mom's cheeks as she wrapped a dishtowel around her hand. She cradled her arm and rocked her body. I got her an ice pack, and she pressed it against the wound to help the pain and stop the bleeding.

At first she didn't talk, and we weren't sure if we should call 911 or Dad.

Charley spoke up. "Should you go to the hospital, Mom?"

"If it doesn't stop bleeding soon, I may need stitches," she said. "Luckily, I got a tetanus shot about a year ago. But I'm afraid of the questions they might ask at the hospital. They might have to report animal bites to state officials. Then I don't know what would happen to Mantha. What have we gotten ourselves into?"

The bleeding stopped after awhile, and Mom assured us that she didn't need to go to the hospital. But the sense of emergency didn't go away. With that bite, everything changed. There had been so many reasons to be afraid *for* Mantha. Now, for the first time, we were afraid *of* Mantha.

"You are all staying inside this afternoon," Mom said, but none of us wanted to go out, anyway. I expected there would be a family meeting that night.

I was wrong. When Dad got home, he said, "You kids go to your rooms so your mother and I can talk." He sounded very serious.

I didn't know what else to do, so I wrote to Libby:

I'm worried about Mantha. She's in a bad mood all the time, sometimes downright mean. Today was the worst. Mantha bit my mother when she tried to pet her. It was just awful. Do you know why Mantha is acting like this?

I got a response in no time:

> I'm really sorry to hear that Mantha bit your mom. That happened to me once, and it was horrible.
>
> I have one idea about what could be bothering Mantha. You may not know the answer to this, but do you think it's possible she could be pregnant? She's very young, but that is the only thing I can think of. A pregnant animal can be moody and erratic.

I rushed to write back:

> Yes! Not long ago, there were about a dozen squirrels chasing Mantha, and a friend said he thought they were trying to mate with her. This explains everything, doesn't it? I thought maybe it was just this muggy Ohio summer. I've been a little crabby myself lately!

I ran downstairs to tell Mom and Dad the news. They would still be worried that Mantha might bite, but at least they would understand why. How could they possibly hold this against her?

"Mom! Dad!" I plunged into the living room, completely out of breath. "I think I know what's going on with Mantha!"

They looked up with a start.

"What is it, Nell? You weren't outside with her just now, were you?" Dad asked, rising from his chair.

"No, but I was online with Libby. She thinks Mantha is

pregnant, which would totally explain why Mantha is acting so crabby!"

"Really?"

"Yes! And I'm sure Libby is right!"

"Why is that?" Mom asked.

"It's kind of a long story," I said, "but wait just a second. I have to get Jack."

I went to the bottom of the stairs and practically screamed, "Jack!"

He came running.

"What's wrong?"

"You have to help me tell Mom and Dad about the day the squirrels chased Mantha."

"Why?"

"Just come on! It's important."

When we got to the living room, Mom and Dad were both standing up, waiting. I had the feeling that I was about to save Mantha's life for the second time.

"This happened a couple of weeks ago," I said, talking a mile a minute, "but we didn't think we should bother you with it at the time."

We told them the story of the Great Squirrel Chase. I was waving my arms and bouncing up and down to demonstrate the excitement. Jack acted out how we held up the sheet safety net, racing around under the squirrels, and how Russ and Joey had seen us and laughed their heads off.

Mom and Dad listened quietly. When we finished, they didn't look as happy or relieved as I had imagined.

"So at the time, you didn't think you should 'bother' us with this information?" Dad's voice was low, but I could tell he was mad. "The neighbors had a ringside seat to you kids stampeding around the yard after a pack of wild animals, but your mother and father don't find out about it until *weeks* later?"

"You didn't know what those squirrels were up to!" Mom added. "What if one of you had been bitten?" She held up her bandaged hand.

"I hope you two understand that it is a serious matter to keep secrets from us," Dad said. "To be sure that you do understand, Jack, there will be no watching the Cleveland Indians tonight. And Nell, no computer. In fact, there will be no TV or computer for the two of you for the rest of the week."

TWENTY-FOUR

Seeing how angry Mom and Dad were over our not telling them about the big chase, I got an idea of what they'd do if they discovered some of the other things I hadn't told them. The *really* big stuff.

The news that Mantha was pregnant did change some things. Mom and Dad let us put food out for Mantha to be sure she got the best nutrition. But there were to be no visits with her. This was not part of our punishment; this was the new house rule. I understood that it was for our safety, but I missed Mantha.

I hadn't heard any police sirens, but I was worried that Mantha could get into more trouble. I saw her out the window a couple of times, but it wasn't enough to know how she was. I looked for a way to see her, even for a few seconds.

Then I got my chance. Mom was called away to a business meeting.

I knew Mom's trust in me had been damaged, and I didn't want to make things worse. But I had to take the risk.

Before she left, Mom told us, "You have plenty of work to keep you busy while I'm gone, and you are all to stay inside. Unless this house is on fire, you are not to take even one step out into the yard. Am I making myself clear?"

This left me a tiny opening.

As soon as Mom was gone, I grabbed a bag of pecans.

"Nell, you aren't going outside, are you?" Charley gasped out the words.

"No."

"Then what are you doing?"

"The screened porch isn't outside, is it?"

"You'll be grounded for the rest of the summer," Jack said. "Maybe the rest of the year! And you'll get Mom and Dad mad at me, too. *You're* the reason I can't even watch TV."

This was a fair argument. I had been asking the boys to lie, or at least to help me keep the truth from our parents. And they didn't even know the whole truth themselves. I felt a new sting of guilt, but I needed their silence. Mantha needed it.

"I was—we were—protecting Mantha," I reminded him.

Jack rolled his eyes and tugged at his cap, but he didn't say anything.

"You could get *Mantha* in trouble if you go out," Charley said. "She might bite you, and then they'll take her and kill her! Don't do it, Nell!" he begged.

"I have to," I said. "I'll be careful."

Charley was right, though. If I was hurt, it would be a nightmare—for me and for Mantha. So even though it was 85 degrees outside, I wore some "armor." I put on blue jeans and a pair of boots. I wore my heaviest winter coat and tied the hood tightly under my chin. I pulled on Dad's thick leather gloves. To top it all off, I put on sunglasses.

While the boys watched from the window, I went out to the porch and cracked the door so Mantha could get in. I called her name and sat waiting, dying from the heat. Luckily, it wasn't long before she heard me. I saw her running down the ash tree. Her back end was wiggling so much that it made me think of a dog wagging its tail. She had missed me, too!

Mantha hopped onto my knee. Maybe she wasn't sure if it *was* me under all those clothes. She jumped onto my shoulder and put her paws on the hood, like she was trying to find my head. I talked soothingly to her, hoping she'd recognize my voice. I put a nut on my shoulder then quickly put my gloved hand back in my pocket. Mantha acted calm and friendly. We visited for about five minutes, and I was sure she had a good breakfast.

Sweat poured off my face and my clothes were soaked, but it was worth it to be close to Mantha and let her know I hadn't forgotten her. I locked the door and went back in the house.

That evening, Mom and Dad called us together.

"When we decided to let you care for Mantha—and Jess—back in the spring, we talked about what a big responsibility it was," Mom said. "We had no idea how big it would get. I guess we thought it would be easy as soon as you didn't have to feed them with a bottle or eyedropper anymore. But there certainly has been a lot more to it, hasn't there?"

We nodded.

"We learned that the hard way," Dad said. "But it wasn't just you kids. Your mother and I went into this without enough preparation. If we had only known then what we know now."

"But we are where we are," Mom said. "There have been bumps in the road, some bigger than others. But, *please*, let's be sure the lines of communication are always open between us. Don't be afraid to tell us anything. We're here for you!"

"Exactly," Dad said. "What upset me the most was that you didn't come to us when you were confronted with a new situation. We're all still learning about Mantha and what is best for her—and us. We need to have all of the facts. You kids can't make decisions on your own about what may or may not be important for us to know."

I squirmed. I didn't think I could stand my guilty conscience for one more second.

"Do you all understand?" Dad asked.

The boys and I nodded.

"Okay, then," Dad said. "With that said, even though it's a few days early, the punishment is officially over. TV and computer privileges are restored."

I didn't deserve my parents being so nice. How could I make it up to them?

Before I got into bed, I checked my e-mail for the first time in several days. There was one from Libby. I'd forgotten what I'd written to her, back when I had been so happy to find out the reason for Mantha biting Mom. Libby said:

> I can't believe that I'm just now learning that you live in Ohio! I live in Ohio, too! Please tell me exactly where you live. I want to come and meet you, your parents, and Mantha!
>
> Can you tell for sure yet if Mantha is pregnant? If she is, an Eastern gray squirrel carries her babies for 40-44 days, so you can figure out her due date. Give her extra food—nuts have

calcium—to keep her healthy and strong. She's
awfully young, but she'll be all right.

I hope to meet you all soon!

I froze. In my excitement about Mantha's pregnancy, I'd
forgotten that I'd been keeping some things about myself—some
important things—secret from Libby. Where I lived was definitely
one of them. Absolutely the last thing I needed right now was for
Libby to come to my house. What could I do? Just stop writing to
her? Tell more lies?

My mind was swimming with ideas. I tried to grab onto one.
Maybe I could say there had been a death in my family. Or that we
were going away on vacation. But those would just be temporary
excuses. And the truth was that I was tired of the secrets and
lies that had grown from the first one. I had ended up lying to
everyone. I wanted it to stop.

I spent a long time writing what turned out to be a pretty
short e-mail:

Dear Libby,

This is very hard to tell you. Last March when
I first wrote to you, I had already decided that I
wanted to keep Mantha as a pet. I would have
done almost anything to make that happen. So I
lied to get your help. I lied about my age, about
where I live, even about my parents. The truth is
that I am 11 years old, and I live in a small town
called Meadowlake. It is not out in the country,
and I probably could have found a wildlife

rehabilitator if I had tried. My parents have been
very concerned all along. I didn't mean to hurt
anyone, especially not the squirrels. I thought I
could help them. I'm sorry.

Your friend (I hope),

Nell

I thought about everything that had happened because of my
lies. I thought about Jess dying, the near disaster with Adrian,
Mom getting bit, the Fleagles. All of this was my fault.

And I thought of something else. Maybe Mom and Dad
would find out about all the lies, too. And they should find out.
From me.

I tossed and turned all night, trying to figure out my next
step and worrying about what my parents and Libby would do
and say.

In the morning, there was a reply from Libby:

I'm hurt, Nell, and I'm very disappointed. I need
some time to think about this.

It was three long, miserable hours before I heard from her
again. Her next e-mail surprised me:

I still want to meet you and Mantha—and your
parents. Would it be all right if I came this
weekend? How about Saturday?

I had no idea what she was thinking. She might even be planning to rescue Mantha from *me*.

But I knew I couldn't say no to her. And I knew what I had to do next.

TWENTY-FIVE

I kept looking for the perfect time and the perfect way to tell my parents. But there wasn't going to be a perfect way, and now I was out of time. Libby was arriving the next day. There would be no more secrets.

It was late in the evening, and Mom and Dad were sitting on the porch talking. I gathered my courage and went outside.

"Guess what?" I started out as if this were the best news ever. "Libby is coming to visit!"

"Oh, really?" Mom said. "That's exciting! When?"

"Tomorrow."

"Kind of short notice, isn't it?"

"It is," Dad agreed. "I know you like this woman, Nell, but I have doubts about her."

"What do you mean, Dad? Libby is great."

"I'm sure she's a well-meaning person. But from the beginning, Libby has set herself up as some kind of expert, and she's let us down. More than once."

"I blame us more than Libby," Mom said to him. "We should have been more involved. We could've found out earlier that she was giving us bad information, and we were heading for trouble. I thought it would be a good project for you,

Nell, but it was too much responsibility—for all of us."

Just when I thought I couldn't feel any worse.

"But doesn't Libby have some accountability, too?" Dad asked. "She's running a Web site and giving out advice."

"Please, stop!" I said. "Libby has tried so hard to help me. I'm the one who passed on bad information. Not Libby."

"What do you mean?" Mom asked.

I dove in headfirst.

"There's a big red notice on Libby's Web site that says if you find a baby squirrel you should take it to a wildlife rehabilitator. I saw it the first day we found Mantha, but I didn't want to give her to someone else. I told Libby I was fifteen years old so she wouldn't think I was too young. I told her we lived way out in the country and that I couldn't get to a rehabilitator. And worst of all, I told her that you two wouldn't help me—that I had to do it all on my own."

The darkening sky didn't hide their stares of disbelief.

"You're saying that you have been lying to us all this time?" Mom asked.

"Not all the time—well, not about everything . . ."

"Is there more?"

"I learned that it's against the law to have native wildlife in Ohio without a permit. That's why I released Mantha early. And the Fleagles and Mrs. Sanchez have been upset about Mantha."

There was silence: a long, cold silence.

Finally, all Dad said was: "Go to your room, Nell. I don't want to talk about this any more tonight."

"I'm really sorry. I—"

"Good night."

On my way inside, I ran into Jack. From the look on his face, I thought he must have heard everything.

"Man!" He stared at me. "What do you think your punishment will be?"

"I'll probably have to stay in my room, in the dark, until I'm eighteen," I whispered. Then I added, "It's my own fault."

"Yeah." Jack nodded. "But I know why you did it. You wanted to help Mantha. And Jess, too."

I went to my room. I was relieved to stop the lies. But it was the worst day of my whole life.

I was the first one up the next morning. I straightened my room, unloaded the dishwasher, and made breakfast for everyone. I didn't think it would change my punishment or make my parents feel any better about things, but it was all I could think of doing.

Right after breakfast, Mom sent the boys to their room with math assignments. Then Mom and Dad and I sat in the living room.

"Nell, I'm at a loss," Dad said. "There's nothing I can say, no punishment I can give, that will make up for what you've done. We're lucky that we haven't had even more trouble. Your mother and I showed poor judgment, too. But Nell, you were reckless and selfish—two words I never thought I'd say about you. You betrayed our trust, and I don't know how you'll earn it back. That's up to you. In the meantime, I want you to have plenty of time to think about it. So, you will not leave the yard or talk on the phone for a month. You will have no Internet access except for monitored schoolwork. Understood?"

I nodded.

"Maybe it's a good thing that Libby is coming," Dad said. "We have a lot to talk about."

"Does she know what's going on?" Mom asked. "The truth, I mean."

I nodded again.

"Is that why she's coming?"

"I don't think so."

But I didn't know for sure.

TWENTY-SIX

When the doorbell rang, I felt like a huge weight was lifted from my shoulders—and dropped into my stomach.

The woman at the door was wearing blue jeans, a plain white T-shirt, and orange high-top sneakers. She was shorter than me and didn't look much older than a teenager. Her long brown hair was pulled in a ponytail, and she had on purple rectangular glasses that made her look cool as well as smart.

"You must be Nell," she said, taking my right hand in both of hers. "I'm Libby."

I instantly felt more relaxed.

I stepped back so she could come into the house.

"Please come in," Mom said.

"Sit down," Dad said. He smiled at her. "Make yourself comfortable."

I was anything but comfortable. I wondered who would bring *it* up first. They covered all the small talk: You have a lovely home. How was the drive over? It looks like rain, but we sure need it.

Then, Dad turned the subject to me. "Nell has been filling us in on what's she been up to. Let me assure you that—"

"Please," Libby put her hand up. "I didn't come here to criticize or blame. Nell and I have been down a long road together. I've had some disappointments lately, but there are things I wish I had done differently, too. For one, I should have insisted on talking to you before I got involved. That's one of the reasons I wanted to come now."

"I know we all have regrets," Mom said, looking at me.

"But I've also learned a lot," Libby said. "People may come to my Web site to learn what to do with an orphaned baby squirrel. But I shouldn't give out that information. From now on, I'll get people to a wildlife rehabilitator, even if I have to locate one myself!"

She looked at me. "Nell made mistakes, but I think she is a remarkable girl."

"Thank you. We agree," Dad said. Then he added, "But we're not going to let Nell off the hook too easily."

"Is there a chance I could meet Mantha before I leave?" Libby asked. "How hard is it to find her?"

I looked at Dad, and he nodded. "Okay. Just for Libby."

I grabbed some pecans, and Libby followed me outside. "Pretty much all we do is call and then wait for her to see us. It shouldn't take long."

We sat on the front steps.

"Libby, I'm really sorry. I never planned . . . I didn't mean to . . . I'm just really sorry."

"I know, Nell," she said. "I'll tell you something. I still remember how it felt when I found my first baby squirrel. That's why I wanted to help you. But I was wrong, too."

I saw Mantha heading toward us. "Like I've told you, she's been crabby. But she should be fine as long as we don't reach out to her."

"Okay."

Mantha put her front paws on my knee, and I gave her a pecan.

"I can tell you right now," Libby said, "she is definitely pregnant. Did you figure out when the babies would be due?"

"I think between August sixth and tenth. If it is on the tenth, that's my birthday."

"That would be wonderful! You'll let me know when they're born?"

"I promise."

Libby took a pecan and held out her open palm. Mantha put her front paws in Libby's hand for a few seconds before taking the nut.

"She's a beauty!" Libby said. "I'm so glad we saved her, Nell."

TWENTY-SEVEN

Mantha's stomach grew big and round. When she stood on her back legs, I could see large dark nipples where there were once tiny pink ones.

Mom and Dad softened a little and decided I could go out to give Mantha extra food if I was careful.

"Put the food on the steps or the ground so she doesn't jump on you," Mom said.

I kept an eye on Mantha, but I was much less involved than we were both used to. I wasn't allowed to hang around with my friends, either. Mom let me make one phone call to Greta to tell her that I was grounded.

"For how long?" she asked.

"A whole month."

"No! It'll be the end of summer before I see you again! What did you do?"

"It's a long story, and this is supposed to be a short phone call." I was kind of glad that I didn't have to explain the whole story to Greta yet.

"This sucks," she said.

"I know. Tell Russ and Joey, okay?"

"Sure. See you next month."

Early in August, I noticed Mantha building a new nest in the thick trumpet vines on the trellis over our driveway. I thought this was a terrible idea. If the babies fell out of the nest—like she and Jess had—they'd fall right onto the concrete driveway. That was bad enough; I didn't even want to think about cars driving in and out.

After she finished the nest, I didn't see her for two days. That was unusual. Several times, I stood under the nest, but I couldn't hear or see anything.

Late on August 6, exactly forty days after The Great Squirrel Chase, I saw Mantha on a tree in the front yard. It was obvious that she'd had her babies: Her back legs had blood on them, and the skin on her stomach was hanging in loose folds instead of pulled tight over a round bulge. I gave her a few nuts, but she didn't stay long.

I ran in the house to spread the news.

"Mantha had her babies!"

"How do you know?" Jack asked.

I described how she had looked.

"How was she?" Mom asked.

"She ate a few pecans, and she seemed okay. She was climbing on the tree, but that was all I saw."

"I guess we'll just have to wait to see about the babies," Mom said.

Since the trellis is right outside the kitchen window, we'd try to watch from inside the house. But the nest was so solid and built so far in the vines that you could hardly spot it. Mantha had certainly learned a lot about nest-building since her first one.

Sometimes, especially around twilight, if we stood underneath the nest, we could hear baby sounds coming from above. Several times, we saw Mantha lying on the trellis right outside the nest, resting with her eyes closed. I guess she just wanted to get away from those noisy, fidgety kids for a few minutes of peace.

My parents gave me special permission to e-mail Libby about the babies. She wrote back:

> That's great! Thanks for letting me know.
>
> I have some news, too. I'm going to graduate school—to become a nurse. I'm closing down the Web site because I'll be so busy.
>
> I've really enjoyed knowing you and Mantha. You take care of yourself, Nell. I hope you never forget all of the things we've learned together. I know I won't.
>
> All the best!
>
> Libby

I thought Libby would make a great nurse, but I was a little sad about her news.

> I will remember, Libby.
>
> Good luck at school. I'll miss you! Thanks for ALL of your help.
>
> Your friend,
>
> Nell

The other thing that happened the month of my grounding was that I turned twelve. We had a small family party—a cookout and cake and ice cream. Mom and Dad bought me a beautiful book to use for my life list. It has a gold cover with a painting of a bluebird. There's a silk ribbon to mark the current page and a little strap to attach a pen. Inside are illustrated pages with space for recording observations about birds you see, such as the time and place, and what the bird looks like—coloring, body shape and size, beak shape—plus its behavior and its call and song. I love it!

I could hardly wait for another trip to Glenecho—or anywhere besides the backyard.

TWENTY-EIGHT

Almost the minute my grounding was over, I called Greta.

"Yay!" she shouted. "Finally! There are less than two weeks left before school starts! Want to go to the pool this afternoon? Joey and Russ are already there."

"Sounds great. Don't tell them I'm coming. We'll surprise them."

I hadn't been to the town pool all summer. My stomach did little flip-flops as I got ready. Was I so excited about going to the pool—or seeing Russ?

"Hey! Look who it is!" Joey yelled when he saw me. "Are you out on parole, Nell?"

I waved.

Russ and Joey got out of the pool, grinning and dripping as they hurried over. They seemed really happy to see me.

We spread towels in a grassy, shaded area.

"Get right to it, Nell!" Joey said as soon as we sat down. "I can't picture you spraying graffiti on bridges or turning over trash cans. What did you do? Start smoking?"

I laughed, but I hadn't figured out how I was going to tell them.

145

"Russ knows a little about this," I said.

"He does?!" Greta's mouth dropped open. "He didn't say anything to us!"

Russ shrugged. "I can keep a secret."

"What?! Spill it, Nell!" Joey said.

"I'm surprised the whole world doesn't know this part, because Constance Fleagle is the one who first told me."

I was still amazed that Constance hadn't gossiped all over town.

"Who listens to her, anyway?" Greta asked. "What could *she* say that would get *you* grounded?"

"That it's illegal in Ohio to keep native wildlife, say, something like a squirrel."

"Whoa!" Joey said. "You *are* a criminal!"

"I guess so."

"Did Constance really know something your parents didn't?" Greta asked. "And what about the woman at the squirrel Web site? She should have known."

"Right," I said, looking down. "Libby *did* know. She told me from the beginning that some states had laws. There's more to it, but basically I never tried to find out if Ohio was one of those states. At least not until Constance came over. That's when Russ helped me find out, and then I released Mantha. But I kept all of this stuff from my parents."

"And me," said Greta.

"I know. I'm sorry. I was trying to make things easier, but I made them worse."

Greta squeezed my hand. "I guess I'm lucky, or I might have ended up grounded, too."

"How did your parents find out?" Russ asked.

"I told them."

They got quiet before Greta said, "Hey! We missed your birthday while you were locked up."

I was grateful she changed the subject.

"It's not too late to celebrate," Joey said. "Let's get some ice cream at the snack bar."

"It's great to have you back, Nell." Russ smiled at me.

I smiled, too.

We had a fun afternoon and went back to the pool every day until school started.

Despite all the problems I'd had over the summer, I was sad to see it come to an end.

One day in September, Dad called from outside, "That squirrel of yours is up to something. She has something in her mouth. Come check it out."

"She's moving the babies!" I said. "She must have a new nest." I'd read that there could be several reasons for this. Maybe there was a problem with insects in the old one, or she could have felt the babies were threatened in some way. Maybe they just outgrew it.

We watched as Mantha crossed the trellis, climbed a vine of ivy up the house, and disappeared over the roof. We ran around the house and saw her jump to a limb of the oak tree. She took the baby into a nest on a high limb and came out a few seconds later. She crossed the roof back to the old nest and came out with another baby. She made one more trip after that.

Once Mantha and her family had moved out of the nest over the driveway, we got a ladder and looked inside. The nest was circular and built mostly from twigs and leaves. There was a soft lining of moss, bark, leaves, fur, even feathers, plus dryer lint and yarn that I had been leaving out for her—some of the things Jess used to like to nest with. There was also a small American flag woven in the side! The stick was missing, but we recognized it as the one Dad had stuck in the flower bed on the Fourth of July.

That was how we knew that Mantha had three babies, but it was the last time that we knew where they lived.

In the fall, we settled back into more intensive schoolwork at home. Plus, just like in the spring, I couldn't seem to get away from baseball as the rest of the family watched the playoffs and World Series. I found other things to keep me busy. I went back to the plans for a family trip to Civil War sites, and it was time to start a new book in my piano lessons. I'd learned that I really liked being outside. I even volunteered more often to help Dad with yard work.

I don't ever remember a fall with so many acorns. Dad had the boys and me rake them up, and we had trash cans full of them. I saved them in the garage to put out during the winter for Mantha. A TV weatherman said that some people believe an abundant crop of acorns is a sign it will be a cold, snowy winter.

The squirrels sure seemed to be preparing for a harsh season. Almost any time I saw Mantha, she was burying nuts in the yard. I wondered how she'd remember where they were. Sometimes, there were three young squirrels playing around her, and sometimes we'd even see the babies out on their own, although they stayed together. But after a few more weeks, we couldn't tell Mantha's babies from all the other squirrels in the neighborhood.

TWENTY-NINE

The forecast for a harsh winter turned out to be right: snowfall was way above average, and the temperatures way below.

Greta is a big fan of snow and cold weather, mostly because it means school might be closed. On the eighth snow day of the year, Greta said, "To celebrate, let's go ice skating. Joey and Russ will be there."

Joey and Greta talked on the phone all the time. Russ and I were becoming good friends, but after that one time I called about the law, we had never called each other again. I wondered if we'd ever be the kind of friends that Greta and Joey were.

Greta got ice skates for Christmas, and she told me I could rent some at the park, where the frozen pond had recently been opened for skating. I was hoping that maybe I'd found my sport. On TV, ice skating looks so easy. I could imagine myself doing it, even though I'd never tried before.

I bundled up in layers of my warmest clothes, including my heavy parka. I reached in my pocket, looking for gloves, and found some pecans. I remembered the summer day I wore the coat out on the porch with Mantha so she couldn't bite me.

It was really cold, but despite the icy roads that had closed school in the morning, by afternoon the weather was perfect. The sky was clear blue, and the sun shining on the snow was almost blinding. As Greta and I walked to the park, it felt like a scene in a movie.

I sat on a bench at the park and laced up the skates, making sure to tug them tightly—"for ankle support," Greta had told me. I pulled myself up, but immediately lost my balance. I tried to land my butt on the bench, missed, and fell over the back of it. I was lying with my feet straight up in the air when Joey and Russ walked up, skates slung over their shoulders.

"Was that a double or triple axel?" Joey asked, leaning over me.

"Ha-ha," I said.

"Want to try that again?" Russ asked, offering me his hand.

Fortunately, my heavy winter clothing had cushioned my fall. Unfortunately, all that bulky material made it hard for me to get back on my feet, especially with the bench and a large bush in the way. I struggled to get up, like a toddler in a snowsuit, nearly pulling Russ over as he tried to help me.

Once I was standing again, I found myself with the same problem—staying that way. My ankles wobbled, and my body swayed.

"Hey!" Greta called from the middle of the ice. "Out here!"

Russ and Joey took off after her.

I had no idea how I would join them.

I got one foot onto the ice, but it didn't want to stay put while I tried to get the other one to meet it. Greta skated over to help me. By leaning on her, I got both feet onto the ice. But as soon as she let go, the top half of my body was propelled backward, and my feet kicked out in front of me. I ended up back on my butt. Greta wrestled me to my feet. This time, I thrashed my arms around and around to keep my head forward. But that only caused me to bend in the other direction. I couldn't seem to get upright.

"Careful!" Greta yelled as she glided off. She might as well have said, "Fly!"

Little kids half my age were skating circles around me. If I could've made my way back to the edge, I would've found my boots and headed for home.

I felt someone grab my elbow, slowing the crazy dance I was doing so I could almost straighten up. I actually saw something besides scratched ice.

"Try to stand up," Russ said.

"What do you think I'm doing? Looking for lost change?"

"Sorry." He laughed. "I'll help you." He slipped one arm around my waist and held my arm with his other hand.

This was definitely better. We went slowly, but after a few times around the pond, I started to get the hang of it.

"Hey, look at Nell!" Joey yelled as he sped by. "Woo-hoo!"

"I think you've got it," Russ said. He let go of my waist and took my hand. I wasn't sure if the tingling in my stomach was from the thrill of skating or the pressure of his hand.

We skated until sunset.

It felt funny to put my boots back on. They made me feel short and slow.

"Did you have fun?" Russ asked.

"It was a blast. Thanks for your help."

"No problem. Hey, I was wondering. . . . Do you think you'd like to go to a movie sometime? I mean, you know, with me?"

It was the first time I'd ever seen Russ nervous. That was the biggest thrill of all.

I said yes.

THIRTY

Through the winter, I saw Mantha only occasionally. Would it be different once it got warm out?

One of my regular spring and summer chores is caring for the flower garden in the front yard. This year, Dad decided to turn the whole project over to me. I spent weeks researching plants and flowers and planning color schemes. I drew up a design and started preparing the ground on a warm day in March. I was outside for an hour or more before Mantha stopped by to see me.

"Hey there, pretty girl," I said. I realized that I'd forgotten to bring any nuts out with me—something that never would have happened last year. I ran inside to grab her a treat, but she was gone when I got back.

Dad came to check on my progress. "Nell, I haven't said anything before, but I'm really pleased by the way you've been pulling back from Mantha. I know it's the best thing for all of us, especially her."

"I think it's her as much as me," I said. "I miss her, though."

"I know. I never told you that I talked to the Fleagles and Mrs. Sanchez," he said.

I looked up, afraid of what he might say next.

"They weren't as upset about the squirrel as you might have thought. In fact, Mr. Fleagle was a little angry at Constance for coming over to talk to you. He told her to mind her own business."

I guess that explained why the whole town didn't know about Mantha. For once, Constance didn't get her way.

I was in the garden every day that wasn't too cold. I couldn't help but think of what a nuisance Mantha had been last summer when I worked in the yard. Whenever I'd try to weed the flower bed, she'd bat at my hand and make grunting noises, scolding me. I finally figured out that she had buried nuts there and was afraid I was trying to take them. Why wasn't she bothering me this year?

One day I figured out that it had been over a week since I had seen her. Panic rose into my throat. I sat on the front steps to catch my breath and take a good look around. She had to be here somewhere.

"Hey!" Russ said, bringing his bike to a stop on the sidewalk. "You look busy."

I smiled, but I guess it wasn't too convincing.

"What's wrong?"

I trusted Russ enough to talk about Mantha. We talked a lot now.

"I haven't seen Mantha in a week."

"Did anything happen?"

"Not that I know of. I've seen her less and less since winter. But this still feels weird. Bad weird."

"I'm sure she'll show up." We sat for a minute or two, then he said, "What are you planting?"

He knew about my project, so maybe he was just trying to distract me from worrying about Mantha—but it worked. I pulled the diagram out of my pocket and started talking about annuals and perennials and shade-loving and sun-loving plants.

Mantha never came back.

I remembered all the bad things we imagined could have happened to Mantha and Jess's mother, why she didn't come back for her babies. But I also knew there could be other reasons Mantha left.

I didn't see her enough to know if she was pregnant again, but it was the right time of year for that. She could be off somewhere preparing for a new family. She certainly didn't rely on me anymore for food. Maybe she'd formed new habits over the winter and was ready to move on—like any other squirrel in the neighborhood.

I'll never know for sure what happened, but I still look for her sometimes when I'm outside.

One day in May, I glanced out the back door and something caught my eye—a blue jay sitting on the basketball hoop. He saw me and cocked his head to the side, watching and waiting.

I went to the cupboard where we'd always kept a stash of nuts for Mantha's visits. There was still a bag of peanuts. I took a few and stepped onto the porch. I tossed one up, and the jay caught it in the air. He cracked it open against the hoop and ate the nut. I threw him a couple more before he flew off.

It was nice to see an old friend stop by to visit.

I know I made a lot of mistakes with Mantha, but I'll always be grateful for my time with her and Jess. I loved them, and they changed my life.

For one thing, I pay more attention to what's going on around me. Because you never know where some little, unexpected thing might take you.

Even the tiniest sound, like the one that led me to Mantha.

Author's Note

What would you do if you found a baby squirrel in your yard? What *should* you do? I hope that, after reading *Nuts*, your answer is to call a wildlife rehabilitator!

If you find any wild animal that is hurt or sick, or an orphaned baby like Mantha and Jess, your first and main concern must be for your own safety. Never walk up to an injured animal—even one that isn't wild—because it might bite you in order to defend itself. Tell an adult!

Next, think about getting help for the animal. That is the job of a wildlife rehabilitator, and there are many ways to find one in your area. The Southeastern Outdoors Web site has a directory of US wildlife rehabilitators (http://www.southeasternoutdoors.com/wildlife/rehabilitators/directory-us.html). Click on the name of your state for a list of organizations or individuals to contact.

If you don't find a person in your area, call or do an Internet search for the Fish and Wildlife (or Fish and Game) department in your state. You can also contact the local animal-control officer, the Humane Society, or a veterinarian to get the name and phone number of wildlife rehabilitation facilities in your city or town.

If you call a wildlife rehabilitator, he or she will tell you how to decide if the animal needs help, and if it does, exactly what to do. Some rehabilitators provide rescue services when that is necessary, but it is likely that you—with a trusted adult, of course—will be given instructions for how to safely bring the animal to the rehabilitator.

The wildlife rehabilitator will examine the animal and decide if it can become well enough to be returned to the wild. If it can, then the animal will be given any necessary medical care, possibly even surgery. It will also receive food and medicine until it is strong and healthy enough to be released. Keep in mind that rehabilitators often provide these services with little or no financial support. A small donation from your family, if possible, would be helpful and appreciated.